CW00255591

DREAM CATCHER

A NOVEL

BY

CHRISTOPHER BIGSBY

For Stephen – without
whom this book wouldn't
have found its way into
print.
Many thanks.

Thanks to Stephen Bennett for all his technical assistance.

CHAPTER ONE: HAM ON RYE

It had been one of those days. Nobody I wanted to talk to wanted to talk to me. I got caught in the rain, dropped a cup of coffee crossing the street and a dollar blew out of my hand at 40th and Broadway. I chased it for half a block and got dog shit on my shoes. Not that I am unused to shit of one kind or another. For a reporter, it goes with the territory. I didn't come from here, but who wouldn't relish a city changing from day to day, a smear of dog shit a small price to pay.

Here was the din of tumbled streets, a mixture of races, sexes, people on the move assuming that upwards was the only direction worth going, fear of a descent into hell long since left behind. Ours is a country with a fondness for the subjunctive, favouring what might be over what is, what we already possess seeming of less value. Becoming rather than being, that is our mantra. If it was to be my future, having journeyed halfway across the continent, so it was for those who travelled steerage over an ocean believing tomorrow must be better than today or why prove traitors to their own history, country, family, religion. I had none of that last. Years of church services and Sunday schools had stamped that out of me, as had people who thought their suffering a sign of God's grace rather than of an indifferent universe.

There were churches galore, along with synagogues, but I soon discovered religion had concluded a deal with ambition, money, desires of one kind or another. No doubt there were rules, but contravention was one of them. With such a clash of nations, languages, accents, beliefs, practices, none took primacy. In a place where everyone was a stranger, no wonder I felt at home.

Admittedly, the streets smelt of manure. They did where I came from, but here there are those who profit from shovelling it up and selling it to the Italians who grow tomatoes and vegetables in Brooklyn. There are others who rent a cart for a dollar to sell their wares, happy to do so in the knowledge they will soon employ others, and so the upward spiral continues.

As they learn a language, or some approximation of it, they buy cheap copies of Samuel Smiles' *Self Help*, believing Horatio Alger Jr. tells the truth, though truth was never of much interest to him, his biography of Garfield being mostly made up. But who wants truth when fiction will serve better and bring in the dollars? The whole point of a dream is that you know it is unobtainable but dream on nonetheless, so I was not surprised when I arrived and secured my first employment, selling newspapers to those who rushed by pursuing happiness while unsure what form it might take. I would hold out a paper and they would place a coin in my hand and carry away news of what was happening here or around the world as if such knowledge was essential in a city that thought itself a world unto itself, wishing to believe that all events, wherever they occurred, existed as a kind of background to their own lives, a reassurance that they were right to leave some other place for this place, where everything, themselves included, was always in the making.

I was doing this job for no more than a month before I chased the papers I sold to where they were made, becoming a runner for those who themselves rushed from the building with a sandwich in one hand as they went in search of news which I quickly discovered was whatever they, and those who employed them, declared it to be. The step from there to becoming one of them was not so difficult that I did not manage it before the end of my first year in this metropolis, this acme of civilisation, if also, as I swiftly discovered, this Sodom, this inferno, this magical, disturbing, invigorating, dismaying, wonderful, paradoxical, alluring, frightening, challenging place.

So, there I was, far from the dust of my distant home that was never a home, paid to explore the enigma that should have been the capital of the Republic rather than some swamp on the Potomac where were gathered the nation's scoundrels and villains to determine what our democracy should be as they counted their dollars rather than their blessings. But that is the South. Here, we are Yankees, though I confess dollars are a measure here, too. What other measure is there?

You think, maybe, New York is people landing at Castle Gardens, staring up at the tallest buildings they have ever seen as someone picks their pockets, a place so hot in summer that those that can leave and those that can't struggle to sleep outside on fire escapes, doors and windows invitingly wide. Then there are the winters. Only two years before I arrived, there had been a snowstorm like none could remember. There were those in tenements who died of the cold. No steam heat for them, and no mercy either. But this is a place where people sign their names to the contract to be found in Shelley's *Prometheus*: 'to hope till Hope creates from its own wreck the thing it contemplates.' I may be a journalist, but I am not ignorant having studied writers for no other reason than I wanted to be one.

Once on the payroll, I started out covering accidents. Someone in the police would let us know, for a consideration, the kind paid on a regular basis, and that suited everyone I was told. Often these involved horses which overall tended to come off better when it came to collisions. Sometimes the word accident was stretching it a bit. A man would be found dead in an alley and if it seemed unlikely the coroner would call it natural causes, on account of the bullet wound or the knife being too cheap for the man who used it to bother pulling it out, it would be said he had accidentally shot himself or fallen on his knife while peeling an orange. Nothing to see. Move on by.

At first, anxious to impress, I asked questions, too many it appeared since my efforts never made it into the paper. Other times, it was suicide and even I couldn't make it anything else. What surprised me was how inventive people could be in giving up on the pursuit of happiness. It was as though jumping from windows, throwing yourself in the river or leaping in front of a train or speeding cab, was altogether too much of a cliché. They would drink liquids designed to clear drains, impale themselves on railings, throw themselves down garbage chutes, though that last seldom worked as they found themselves in bins alongside every disgusting thing that those in the apartment building chose to throw away. Another man swallowed a whole bag of nails and a broken razor. You've got to be desperate to do that unless you wanted a piece in the paper. He got one. People like to read about that sort of thing.

I would find myself in places like Blind Man's Alley at 26 Cherry Street where the landlord, Daniel Murphy, fought to stop those who would force him to make the place liveable arguing that the blind don't care if the place is dark, they not being able to see the conditions they live in. You might think there's no crime in Blind Man's Alley? The place is a crime in itself. And if being blind might make you vulnerable it could also be an advantage when begging.

And it's no better on Park Avenue South, this sounding better than Fourth Avenue which it was only a couple of years ago. Everyone changes their names here so why not a street. I'd covered a murder in the Park Avenue Hotel on 31st Street, human nature and the human body being much the same anywhere so that an ice pick will have the same effect uptown as down and in both cases it could be described as an accidental death if it served someone's purpose. Reality was whatever someone wanted it to be in 1890.

After a while, though, I began to get interested in the suicides that weren't suicides and in those who made them look as though they were, not always very convincingly, or even caring. Then there was the general weirdness. A man decided to kill his ex-wife. I don't know why since it turned out he had gone off with several women himself. Anyway, he rigged up a shotgun with a length of string going to the door of his apartment so that anyone coming through would be blown apart. Dangling the prospect of money to support his daughter, he persuaded her to come round. Turns out she hated him so much she refused, instead sending the daughter since she had no money and needed it whatever he was like. So, the daughter arrived and found the door partly open. As a result, she took the full blast. When I got round the blood was still oozing down the wall. They tracked him down, but he shot himself. Was that so he wouldn't be taken in or because, however much he hated the wife, he maybe loved his daughter? Everyone said he was a quiet man, not knowing, presumably, of his habit of collecting women. After that, I looked at people differently when I passed them on the street. When I was told we are made in God's image it made me wonder which God they were talking about and how long before he might choose to kill the lot of us.

You can only deal with this kind of stuff for a while before it begins to get to you, so I began to cover politics. I would be there when an alderman announced he was running for office, or even someone whose ambitions stretched to Albany in one direction and Washington in the other. They all said the same thing. How do you make a grab at power and what it brings to you if you don't candy it over with an abstract noun or two, preferably freedom, democracy? And to a man they were going to stamp out corruption, speak up for those whose voices were not heard, clean the stables, except you could take side bets on how long before they found themselves in court for paying back the favours they were granted by those who wanted a return on their dollars.

You'll be thinking I'm cynical, but that's because you're not a reporter. You maybe like to be lulled to sleep by politicians' promises. I get it. We would all rather believe in what Presidents say in State of the Union speeches. We are good. We are the best. We are the envy of the world. The future is bright, within our grasp. We are one people, sharing the same dream.

If I was glad to be taken off the politics beat, I was equally glad when I was asked to switch to corruption, though in truth that often meant the same thing. It was a relief, though, not having to write down what some candidate or other said, knowing he knew as well as I that it was like a pacifier for a baby. And when they went out and voted for him that made me think about the people I was writing for. If they preferred lies rather than painful truths, then what was I up to?

I saw some of the letters they wrote, often in green ink, sounding off about anything that occurred to them, objecting to articles that failed to echo what they thought, or thought they thought. Some of them had to have their spelling and punctuation corrected before they could be printed, yet they were The People and this was a democracy in which every crazed person got to vote when some of them had difficulty writing their own names let alone having the first idea what the issues might be. Well, I guess we are all conspirators in that.

I've stopped people on the street to ask them their opinion about almost anything and there would be this pause as their brains tried to get going. We are supposed to be a nation of Washingtons, Jeffersons and Lincolns but when I mentioned them a fair number of those I stopped would look at me dumbly as if these were the names of some sportsman they had failed to register. Enough. I suspect all countries are the same while those we think the smartest are incapable of washing a shirt being too busy figuring how to beat everyone else to the prize, even if they don't quite know what that is beyond hard cash and the power they presume it will bring.

Anyhow, there I was, with shit on my shoes, back in the office and with what passed for a cup of coffee in my hand, thinking I was safe, until I got the call. It was only the second time I had been invited up to his apartment, invited being maybe altogether the wrong word. I was used to doing what I was told downstairs by a man with eyeglasses, printer's ink on his hands, and the social graces of an orang outang. 'Go here! Don't go there! Get me the story, get me ham on rye and hold the mayo!' Maybe not the ham on rye anymore, though when I first came through that frosted glass door and saw desk after desk and paper everywhere, not knowing who was who or what was what or how to write a decent sentence, then I used to go for ham on rye.

I soon learned, though, that he answered to someone else, the someone else who owned the paper and who lived above the shop, which is to say he had an apartment on an upper floor and sent down messages to the editor telling him how he was to do his job so he could tell us how to do ours. No one knew much about him beyond he got his money from his father who got his from his father who had some scheme it was best not to know too much about. Dirty money cleans itself as it cascades down the years. Actually, dirty money is always clean so long as it gets washed by the right people.

We claimed to be a crusading newspaper though our crusades weren't of the Christians taking Jerusalem kind. Mostly, we had campaigns to lower the drinking age or have the Governor's birthday made a public holiday, though we did, every now and then, chase after corrupt aldermen provided they were the right corrupt aldermen and not the ones we supported who by definition weren't corrupt. You'd have to be stupid not to see who we favoured. Every now and then there would be an editorial explaining that we were for the people, apple pie, God, redistricting, whichever seemed most likely to add a few thousand to our circulation, not that we could compete with the *World* with its crime stories and stunts, though Dana, on the *Sun,* liked poking Pulitzer in the eye.

Pulitzer, who owned the *New York World*, was a Jew born in Hungary who spoke three languages, not including English, so that he fit right into New York. When he started as a reporter he was known as Joey the Jew, though Dana preferred Judas Pulitzer. A one-time Republican, he joined the Democrats, so he covered the waterfront. He turned the *World* round discovering that crime, scandal, disasters were what readers wanted, and I guess the *Telegraph* attempted to out-crime, out-scandal, out-disaster it. One difference was that Cobb at the *World* was known to have stand-up arguments with Pulitzer while our own Fickey never won, as far as I knew, though he had a way of losing that could turn out to be winning in the end.

Nobody saw much, if anything, of the man upstairs. He was above us in more ways than one. Papers have to be owned by someone, though, and it hardly made a difference to me. I went where I was sent and, for the most part, didn't go where I was told not to. That didn't make me spineless, only aware of who was paying me, though there was a certain latitude it must be said because in the end we were all judged by the bacon we brought home. Get a story on the front page and nobody asked how you got it as long as it stood up or stood up for a day or two by which time most readers had lost interest, so it followed we did, too.

Now here I was, climbing the stairs and knowing, even then, that it had to do with Indians because it was always to do with Indians. 'That's America's story' he used to say each Christmas, which was the only time anyone ever saw him, unless you caught him off to the theatre, tails flying, cigar glowing red like a beacon. The only Indian I had seen was Sitting Bull in a show back in '84 as part of something called Sitting Bull's Combination, at the Eden Musée waxwork museum. I only went to amuse a girl I was thinking of maybe, well, just maybe. She wasn't amused. Then there was the photograph of him and the fraudster Buffalo Bill whose life was made up for him by Ned Buntline in a dime novel, the two of them costumed up and standing in front of a backcloth that would have shamed a theatre which is what they were. It was taken in Canada, which seemed right because that was where he ran away across the border. I heard where originally he had been called Jumping Badger, which hardly matched the man behind Little Big Horn, supposing he had been there, as perhaps he hadn't.

Anyway, no one seemed much interested in Little Big Horn and Custer anymore. He even got to meet Grover Cleveland, which was punishment enough.

I read where he had been a member of something called The Silent Eaters, which would have disqualified the editor of the *Telegraph* who could spray his food like a dog marking its territory. That was about it as far as Indians were concerned. They were out there in the Black Hills or Montana or somewhere no one in their right minds would want to be, killing people and smoking pipes, which was fine with me since I never met any on 12th Street.

I got to interview Cody once, if you could call it an interview when all he wanted to do was tell a story I had heard before about how he killed his first Indian at the age of eleven, tangled with the Mormons, was a Pony Express rider, acted as guide, killed thirty-six buffalo in half a mile and countless Indians, scalping some. That last was said boastfully as if he failed to understand that savagery evidently existed on both sides. Happily, we were interrupted so that I was saved from being bored by a familiar recitation. None of it was worth putting in the paper, and none of it appeared.

My subject was New York and those who schemed, robbed, got by one way or another. There were killings alright, but not of those wearing warpaint, unless you count young girls, their faces smeared with rouge, discarded like refuse, such luck as they ever had finally having run out. There were pioneers, to be sure, but they had no need to join a wagon train. Their territory was a city and their journey up through the ranks, criminals becoming politicians as politicians had already become criminals. Those who went west were looking for free land. Here, nothing was free. Everything was for sale.

CHAPTER TWO: A JOURNEY TO NOWHERE

It had been Indians that other time, and a story that came apart in my hands, futile written all the way through it, like the candy at Coney Island. Even then, when I wasn't what I liked to think I am now, the *Telegraph*'s number one reporter, I tried to turn it down. But one look at his eyes, which glowed as red as his cigar, and I knew to change my mind, spin on a dime, and announce that it was what I had always wanted. As if anyone could have wanted to go off with some missionary to a place where there was no whisky and precious little water and no one who gave a shit about anything. But no wasn't an answer you could give, not that I could give, still clawing myself up from ham on rye.

So, it was off to Boston to meet a man who should have been a mortician, dressed, as he was, in black and with eyes that seemed to stare through you to the other world, but in fact was an agent for a bunch of missionaries who had thought to translate the Bible into some God-awful savage tongue and present it to those they wished to save for eternity, whether they wanted such or not, missionaries never being particular on that point in my experience. And there were politicians who thought it a good idea, too, being cheaper, overall, than sending men with guns and horses, men who might want to be paid, guns that had to be bought. The idea was to civilise them with the Bible, though as I recalled that was full of people smiting one another when they weren't begetting.

I had acquired not so much a distrust or contempt for religion as a mild amusement. What, after all, was I to make of Saint Teresa de Avila, founder of the Barefoot Carmelites who fell ill and was cured by potatoes? She developed a habit of levitating and hence had to be held down by several strong nuns. Seventh Day Adventists live longer than the likes of you and me, but the price they pay is to be Seventh Day Adventists. This is a country where people will believe anything. Ponce de Leon looked for the fountain of youth, for some reason in the swamps of Florida. The Adventists' Second Coming hasn't come, and the Spaniard died before reaching fifty. There are those who think that a total stranger on 42nd Street with three playing cards and the smile of a jackal wants to give them money.

And what of the Jews? They can't eat rabbits or pigs and can't drink wine unless it is produced by Jews. There are Jews who make wine? And they can't work on their sabbath, except that if they obeyed that no women's coats would be made on the Lower East Side.

Anyway, apparently in the service of God, or more likely of those with nothing better to do, we set out, by train at first, not so bad if you weren't travelling, as I was, with a man who thought that taking a drink in the smoker was one step away from murdering infants. Even then, it would be a poor reporter who hadn't taken precautions and laid in his own supplies. But the train only took us as far as St Joseph, Missouri, which is far enough when your bottle has run out a few hundred miles further east. Then it was a wagon supplied by some others who were about the business of saving Indians, such as they hadn't shot already or poisoned with the smallpox. We had nothing to do but climb on board and flip the reins, though neither of us did that, there being one of those heathen themselves, who could do that, with a black jacket just like the missionary's and a stove pipe hat that would have looked good on Abraham Lincoln but didn't look at all good on someone whose pigtail stuck out the back, and would, no doubt, as soon have scalped me as given the time of day, which he didn't, not speaking a word the whole time we were with him. You can tell I don't warm to Indians.

And so we travelled, with the Indian chanting to himself, and not in words as far as I could tell, and the missionary singing hymns as though they were in a competition, and I would get to declare the winner. Well, I couldn't have picked the winner, but I knew the loser right enough, and that was me, swaying from side to side, with dust in my mouth and the sun beating down and two crazy people determined to show just how crazy they could be.

Eventually we came to what I assumed was where we were going, which turned out to be nowhere at all. There were a half dozen wooden shacks, one of which sold whisky I was glad to see, and no sight of any other Indians, which was all right by me. Then our Indian stops his chanting and points on out into a territory that seemed as if it had never produced a single living thing, not a blade of grass, a crawling creature or even a snake which would own up to it. And what did the other do, this mortician pretending to be saving souls? He unhitched the wagon, cut out the three horses and we set off right away, before I had a chance to sample what they might chose to call whisky in this excuse for a town.

We rode until sundown. There was nothing there, except a howl of grey dust that spun in little funnels across the ground. And there was nothing to eat or drink and nothing to make a fire out of. So, we lay under the stars, with our heads on our saddles, while he gave out some prayer about bringing light to dark places. Well, he picked a dark place right enough because there were clouds which blotted out the stars so that there was nothing to see and nothing to do except go to sleep and hope to wake up again without having been stung, or bitten to death, in the night. He never spoke much beyond saying 'that way,' or 'fucking flies,' God having not sunk quite as deep in him as he made out, but, then, this country wasn't made for people, and if there were Indians out there, I couldn't begin to think why we had been working so hard to steal their land. They were welcome to it, as far as I could see, which wasn't far by then since I was squinting so much from the sun that what I thought were mountains turned out to be eyelashes. I exaggerate, but not by much, my eyes being used to focussing only as far as the other side of the street, or a bar in poor light.

And in case you thought I was used to riding horses then you've forgotten I come from New York. We got horses there, all right, and I've ridden in a carriage or two and watched where people trot along beside the river. But apart from once sitting on a pony for a minute or so when I was young and knew no better, I had never, never, never, ridden, for mile on mile, through dust and dirt most of which ended up in my under shorts grinding my groin to bone meal. The first night I slept with my legs wide open because, whatever I did, they refused to recognise any kind of kinship that would bring them closer together.

We travelled on again in the morning, until we came to this tent, right in the middle of nowhere. In fact, nowhere would have been a more definite address than this one. There was no good reason I could think of why anyone would have chosen to pitch their tent, or tepee, or whatever, in this place as opposed to any other. But this was where we had been heading, apparently, because the heathen threw his reins to the side, tilted his hat and went to sleep, doubtless having had as little of that commodity as me in a night that was colder than the Brooklyn morgue I used to visit on a regular basis, hoping to pick up a story or two from the various bodies carried in there and dumped on a marble slab, limbs flopping about.

Out in front of the tent sat what I guessed to be an old woman, older than old since the skin of her face seemed to have been folded up ready to put away in some cupboard. I could tell it was likely a woman from the clothes she had on but nothing else would have given it away. You could have had all your arms and legs cut off and your face pushed in and still have felt you had the edge on her when it came to looks. She was staring ahead as if she had her eyes fixed on something that never moved. There was a feather in her hair, but I've seen better on roast chicken in Delaney's where they move food so fast that if you listen hard you can still hear the chickens squawking even as you're cutting off a piece.

He lifted down the Bible, written in her language, and carried it over as if he expected her to leap up in the air and sing a verse of 'My Old Kentucky Home.' But since she had her eyes closed by now, she wasn't exactly impressed. In fact, she might already have been dead for all I knew, for all he cared, holding that book like the infant Jesus himself. And what if she had been looking? If they didn't have a written language, then all she would have seen would have been this big book full of marks.

That didn't matter to her, though, since it turned out she was dying even as he was showing it to her. We neither of us knew it then, looking to see if she recognised just how significant it was to have thousands of years of just talking turned into printed words. After all, they had been here long before any of us, long before ham on rye or Coney Island candy, not knowing how uncivilised they were until we came along and told them before shooting most of them to make our point. But what do you make of people who never wrote anything down, thought they could survive without newspapers, for God's sake, or sewing machines? They were a glimpse into the past that had somehow refused to stay there.

I don't even know if anyone had bothered to tell her that folks in Boston had been shouting Indian words at each other and then finding ways to write them down, giving her and her tribe what they lacked, even if they didn't know they lacked it. Like sin. Whoever knew about that until people set themselves to tell us that what our instincts yearned for, our souls despised.

Anyway, it didn't turn out to matter overmuch whether she knew we were coming, or not, whether that committee of men in black in some Boston clapboard had done what they had done or not, for within half an hour of us getting there she fell slowing sideways, like a tree being felled, her eyes two frosted plums. And that was that.

She was the last member of her tribe, it turned out, though no one had bothered to mention this to me until then. Even if they had I suppose I would still have been sent. Made a better story. There was a story, of course. This would bring a smile to the faces of ninety per cent of the brotherhood as they stood among the sawdust, cradling a glass of Irish. For here were these missionaries who had put the Bible into a language that no one had seen before and no sooner had they done so than the last person on earth who could have been expected to make anything of it at all, even supposing she could, which she couldn't, not knowing what these marks could mean, had chosen that moment to die. So now there was no one who could make any sense of it except those white people back in Boston who had learned the language in order to figure out how to write it and now had only themselves to talk to. The book might just as well have been wiped clean, all those black marks taken off, the slugs of hot metal turned back into molten lead.

And what happens when a language dies? What if there were nobody left who spoke English and there were nothing to show what a great civilisation we had been? No signs saying EATS, or NO SPITTING or BONDS BOOT BLACK IS BEST. Would history die? Would things never have happened if there was nothing showed they had, nothing written that would say people loved and died and knew about beauty and sighed at the moon?

And that was the story that it turned out I had been sent so far to write. It wasn't just a bunch of missionaries who now had a story that had untold itself. I wrote what seemed to me a pretty funny piece. It got spiked. Then I tried it again, as if it were a symbol of something or other, except that I could never figure out what that thing might be. It got spiked again. It seemed that wasn't what the man upstairs had had in mind when he had first summoned me up amongst the mahogany and leather to send me out where he couldn't go himself, as if I were no more than an extension of his faith, his belief, in some future in which red and white men trod the prairie together spouting gospel verses at one another. Well, it hadn't worked out so well and it was as if he and I had some guilty secret we shared, and my part of the bargain was simply to keep my mouth firmly shut. Which I was pleased to do, and I can't say that my career did anything other than blossom, as though somebody up there really did look out for me, as if I were a Mason who had tipped him the wink.

On that futile journey I saw a lot of space and came to feel that space was maybe what it was all about, what made the difference. And I would never have learned that where I was. Seeing right to the horizon did something to people, changed their sense of themselves and the place they lived. Things seemed possible that didn't in the city, different possibilities, even if they hadn't to me when I was growing up back in Kansas and space seemed what stood between me and my life.

Riding beside that crazy Indian, and someone who thought the whole world should sing the same song, taught me something else as well. It taught me that there is more than one song, and it pays to acknowledge it. And seeing that woman sitting in the middle of nowhere told me something else. She didn't feel she owned anything in particular since she owned it all, or her share of it. So long as she was alive, it was a place. The moment she died we were in the middle of a wilderness. There was nothing but land stretching off in every direction. She had made it somewhere instead of nowhere. And when she was gone it disappeared. Like time before there was man.

CHAPTER THREE: INDIANS

After a while I was sent off to cover a triple murder in the Bowery and nobody mentioned Indians to me again, except here I was climbing the stairs, with their mahogany bannister, toward the door of the paper's proprietor, knowing, as sure as sure, that he was going to send me off again to study some Indians because they were the country's story. And though now I thought of myself as pretty well someone when it came to reporting, with my name up there so that people could see I was beyond fetching sandwiches for the editor, I knew I was going to have to say yes to whatever madness he suggested because no one said no to him and worked much anymore, and not only on this paper, either.

I knocked, leaning forward respectfully, trying to hear if he had said anything. There was no sound, except somewhere far away the buzz from the street, a horse objecting to being beaten, no doubt, and what sounded like a church bell, though why one should have been tolling was beyond me unless it was welcoming the dead to an afterlife where people didn't beat their horses or send others on crazy errands. I knocked again. This time I did hear something, a feeble cry, and, taking it for permission to enter, took hold of the brass door handle, turned it and pushed. You could smell the money. It was partly cigars, partly leather, partly expensive liquor, partly power. If you had bottled it, it would have sold for a fortune on Wall Street.

At first, I could see little enough. The heavy burgundy curtains were drawn against a daylight that was feeble enough once it had been filtered through the smoke from a few thousand chimneys and tens of thousands of cigarettes. There was a fire in the grate, burning blue and yellow, its flames making the shadows jump. It wasn't winter, but it evidently was in there.

Then I saw that he was seated in a chair whose wings all but concealed him. A hand reached out, pale and thin, and waved me toward another chair, not at all as grand and just beneath a lamp so that he could see me while remaining himself in deep shadow.

'So,' he said, 'she died.'

I pride myself on being fast enough, having to make sense out of the garbage most people speak when a reporter holds a notebook under their nose, but I could make nothing of this.

'Died.' I said, trying not to inflect the word but to leave it there for him to make such sense of as he could.

'Before she could read it.'

'Before she could read it,' I echoed, seeing that this might be my best course, after all. And then, of course, it did make sense to me, if you could call it sense to pick up a conversation first begun years before quite as if I had just made my contribution and then wandered off for a year or two before wandering back to see what he might wish to add to my own remark.

'The Indian?' I ventured.

'Never read it.'

'Never read it,' I echoed, then realised what he meant. Never could have done, I thought, for how on earth could anyone have supposed that the mere act of turning words into marks on a piece of paper would enable a woman who had never seen such to make any sense of it at all. Clearly, they had known they would have to teach her her own alphabet quite as if her own language were strange to her, as doubtless it would have been once it had been swallowed and regurgitated by Boston clerics who had seen no more of Indians than could be picked up from the wooden ones outside cigar stores. But that he should think the woman might ever have been able to make anything at all out of a Bible that did no more than press her into the grey soil already waiting for her was beyond me. And this was the man who shaped the opinion of millions of New Yorkers every day, always assuming them to have no opinions of their own, as did not seem likely to anyone who has tried to have a shave in peace in a barber store.

'That was ...' I paused, unsure to what extent he was indeed deranged and therefore might take against being reminded of what year we were in ... 'some time ago.'

'Exactly!' he said, with a crispness that suggested that he suspected irony on my part. 'Now you must go again.'

Again? Had the woman risen from the grave? Had those clerics been busy once more, spreading the good news of our eternal damnation to those previously unaware of the nature of what awaited them? And as for Indians, I had thought everyone had pretty much given up on them. After the Little Big Horn they had slipped off the front page and most of the other pages as well. Besides, I wrote for people who regarded anything west of Hoboken as having no interest at all, doubting, as they did, that anyone in that territory could even speak English, fondly imagining they did themselves, an illusion which they somehow sustained in the face of ample evidence to the contrary. It was Terra Incognita and incognita was how they fancied it staying.

'I want you to go out there.'

A younger, less experienced man than I would have made the mistake of asking where this 'there' could be but, knowing it would make very little difference, and that I was as good as on my way already, I merely nodded and repeated, 'out there,' still acting on the assumption that saying his own words back to him was the only strategy and that it anyway forestalled any possibility of contradiction.

'Out where?' he asked, thus disproving my thesis.

'To … where it is I must go.'

'Exactly,' he replied, as if I were speaking sense, which even I still had enough sense to know I was not.

'They're dancing again.'

'Dancing?'

'Again.'

Then I recalled where some Indians somewhere or another had got to dancing for some reason that escaped me. My observation may be sharp; my memory is total crap. Apparently, it had been headline news but I never read the headlines, my pieces being placed rather more discretely several pages in so that whoever might take offence would have to read further than most of them were capable of doing.

'Something's happening again.'

A hand reached out and picked up a silver cigar case. There was a blaze of sparks from the fire. I figured my job was to keep my mouth shut, mostly because opening it wasn't going to accomplish much, except possibly get me fired if I told him what I really thought about him and his Indians. He flipped it open and took a cigar out, closed the case, replaced it on the table, clipped the end off then lit it from the stub of the one he had been smoking, the first time I ever saw someone chain smoking cigars.

'Got much on?'

Got much on? I always had enough on to run me ragged. It wasn't company policy to employ enough people to get the job done. I was working on a story or two about graft. There was always a story or two about graft running in the *Telegraph*, though never big enough to disturb any of those who built their careers on it. We didn't exist to change the system. We were a part of the system. Then I was due for a trip up to Hartford that I wasn't looking forward to overmuch, except, since it was a dinner I was covering, there was a chance of a drink or two.

'Yes,' I said, 'a few stories.'

'New York,' he said.

'New York,' I tried.

'This is one town.'

It certainly was. One town.

'Yes, one town.'

He lowered his cigar and leaned forward so that I had the benefit of seeing his sallow face up close. I figured maybe I was overdoing this echo technique.

'But the real American,' he said, eyes glinting in the firelight, 'is out there.'

'Right,' I said, though I didn't really need to bother since he plainly didn't require any contribution from me.

'The real American is the Indian. You know …'

There was a pause, and I began to think that the word he was looking for was my name, though he could have read it every day in his own newspaper.

'… you know, the real American is the Indian.'

'The Indian,' I repeated, taking a chance on it.

'How much you think a hunter can get himself for a buffalo skin?'

It so happened I knew the answer to this, which was just as well since I hadn't really followed a word he had said up to then. I knew it because I had read it in the *Telegraph* only the week before, which is where I guess he had read it, too.

'A buck a throw,' I said, and then 'a dollar each,' in case he didn't speak American, not being Indian as far as I could see but having an accent I couldn't place except it belonged on another continent.

'A dollar each, exactly. And do you know how much it has cost our government to kill each Indian?'

I hadn't the vaguest idea, and to tell the truth I doubted there were many down there in Washington who spent much time working such things out.

'A dollar,' he said, and leaned back in his chair as if he had just come up with the second law of thermodynamics. 'A dollar.' Case closed.

'Well,' I said, 'a dollar,' not being sure whether he reckoned that cheap or expensive.

'That's the price we put on human life.'

Ah, so the *Telegraph* was about to come out in favour of Indians. Well, I couldn't see that boosting circulation over much. Tell the truth, another Little Big Horn would have done that rather better. But it wasn't my job to make calculations like that. All I did was turn in copy by the inch.

'Just a dollar,' I said, trying to get the right inflection.

'Just a dollar.'

'Not too much for a buffalo pelt, either,' I added, not sure, to tell the truth, whether they were called pelts or not, the closest I ever got to buffalo being the steaks I ate at Sharkeys on 41st Street.

There was a silence and I got to listen to the wood crackling away in the grate while I figured if I had put a foot wrong. Then I began to feel as if he might have had a stroke, since he didn't say any more. I thought of trying one more, 'Just a dollar,' to see if that might get him started again but figured in the end to keep quiet.

'I want you to go out there,' he said, finally. 'Take a photographer. Go out there and bring me the story.'

'Sure,' I said, 'absolutely.' He was plainly completely off his head, but there you are. He was a millionaire who was off his head and that made all the difference.

'You know what the story is?'

'Absolutely,' I said, not having the faintest idea but understanding where my paycheck came from, that being all the sense of direction I needed. 'Precisely,' I said, and then 'exactly,' in case precisely wasn't quite precise enough.

'It's the Indian.'

'Right. The Indian.'

'Know where they come from?'

'The Indian?' I asked, checking we were still on the same planet.

42

'They walked. Didn't have the horse back then.'

'No horses, eh?' I didn't know one person who could give a shit where the Indians came from or whether they had horses or not. And I certainly wasn't that one.

'God's people.'

God's? If they were God's people, I wanted to ask, where was he when the US Army was kicking the shit out of them?

'Do you know Thoreau's last word?'

Something about ponds for a bet.

'Indians,' he said.

'Indians?'

'Indians.' He said this as if it were a logical thing for some New Englander to say.

'Well, that's quite … something.' What else was I to say.

'I want photographs. Like in the Civil War.'

The Civil War, no less. That was the way they were in the papers. They thought all history was staged just for them. And they weren't beyond giving history a helping hand if it didn't seem about to oblige with stories big enough.

'The Civil War?' I allowed a tinge of scepticism into my voice, committing myself to a rising inflection before I had time to stop it. He leaned forwards again, his pale face swimming out of the gloom.

'Sitting Bull took a photograph you know.'

Well, that was good to know. It's always worth having a hobby, even if he was known for slaughtering soldiers and anyone else he had a mind.

'How long until the end of the century,' he asked.

This was the kind of easy question I appreciated. 'Ten years.'

'Armageddon,' he replied, sorting things out neatly for me since I had already been to interview half a dozen or more cranks who were looking forward to being annihilated in just over a decade's time and couldn't wait for the buildings to fall, the dead to rise and funeral parlours to pay ten cents on the dollar to investors. Already, out there in Hartford, there were insurance companies counting the greenbacks from those smart enough to bet on the apocalypse but not smart enough to ask themselves how they were going to benefit from it when the oceans of the world closed over their heads.

'Time was when our dates didn't mean much to the Indian.'

The Indian again.

'But one of the blessings we gave them, along with Christianity, was a knowledge of the calendar and the time piece. They don't read the Bible like you or me.'

He was fifty per cent wrong there, but I wasn't about to point that out to him.

'They read a bit here and they read a bit there and there are those of them who have strung the pieces together and they see the end of time. They figure that now is the moment to settle accounts. Figure it out.'

I had been trying to since opening the door, and all I had figured was that I would be packing such as I possessed sometime in the near future to travel out to some as yet undetermined part of the Great American Desert to watch a bunch of Indians dance and welcome in the next century. But since that was some way off, I was uncertain as to how long this assignment would last. My one hope was Mike Fickey, Editor, son of a bitch and practised hand at frustrating the various orders that descended from this apartment from time to time. I could already hear what he would say to me, and I figured the chances of me ending up in some cow town watching Indians do the two step were remote enough for me not to get too concerned as yet.

'Know why I chose you?'

I didn't, unless it was that last fiasco when another Indian had decided it was a good time to die.

'Because you write pictures. Pictures are good. Why else we pay people to take them. But you can't beat the right word in the right place. Those are the kind of words you write.'

Well, I hadn't come looking for an endorsement
and, truth to tell, I would have traded it in for not
climbing those stairs to get this wildness poured in my
ear, but, then, my every day was filled with strangeness
of one kind or another. If it weren't for strangeness
there wouldn't have been a *Telegraph* and I wouldn't
have had a job to keep me in liquor. Also, if I wrote
pictures how come he talked about photographs which
were all staged anyway, especially when it came to
Indians who looked as though they were tailor's
dummies nailed to the floor, having been Christianised
to death, or ravaging savages who somehow found time
to stop ravaging so they could pose while a man
disappeared under a black cloth and looked at the world
upside down. Look in a man's eyes in a photograph and
he is dead. Nothing there. Meet him or her in the flesh
and chances are the eyes will tell you if he'll buy you a
drink or stab you in the throat. Not always, though. I
have looked in eyes and seen nothing but a cold
darkness. That's why they were employed by those who
preferred others should persuade people to do what they
were told. Their souls had been surgically removed at
birth.

Then, when I was expecting no more than to be dismissed, he rose from his chair and walked across to a bookcase. I assumed it might be fake. You can buy them by the yard to impress the illiterate, and most of the rich are such as far as I can see. But he picked a book, already sticking out a little from among the others, and brought it to where a light spilled a pool of gold. He opened it.

'Do you know what this is?' he asked.

I was tempted to say, 'a book,' just in case he was testing me, but I thought better of it, not least because he was jabbing his finger at the gold lettering on the spine, albeit upside down from where I was so that there was no way I could tell what it was.

'No? This is the Doctrine and Covenants of the Mormon Church.'

'Right,' I said, as if sane people could be expected to flourish that from time to time.

He opened it at a page which had a piece of paper sticking out and read in a wavering voice, '"Second of April 1843. I was once praying very earnestly to know the time of the coming of the Son of Man, when I heard a voice speak the following: "Joseph, my son, if thou livest until thou art eighty-five years old, though shalt see the face of the Son of Man." The Messiah, you see.'

I did, indeed. He was cracked beyond repair.

'Which year is this?'

I paused, suspecting a trick, but then figured there was no harm in confirming the date. '1890.'

'Right. Last month, March, he came. The Messiah.

My God, and I missed it. Maybe it was in the *World*.

'Or at least word has reached me that makes me think it possible. What do you think? The Indians say next year. That's the dance. The whites will all disappear, and the Indian dead will rise.'

What did I think? I preferred next year if we were all going to die, and dead people would be roaming around. In truth what I really thought was that the sooner he was taken where people could look after him and make sure he could do no damage to himself or others, the better we should all be. Meanwhile, I hunted for a reply, but happily he did not need one, carrying on after the shortest of pauses.

'He has appeared to the Indians, who tend the vineyard, who were led to Zion and have the power of the Latter Days. He appeared, I am told, at Walker's Lake, in the presence of those from many tribes. Did you know that the Book of Mormon was translated and given to them? Three years ago, in Spanish.'

In Spanish? Why not Swahili? Did Indians speak Spanish? Then again, he was talking about a bunch of people who dug plates out of the ground and said they were the word of God, so why the hell not Spanish or any other language come to that. I'd heard it was ancient Egyptian, though the absence of ancient Egyptians made that hard to verify. And was that maybe what I was supposed to be doing, those years ago? Bringing them news of the Second Coming? It seems I was carrying the wrong book to the wrong people.

'And the word is spreading.'

All the way up to the third floor of a Manhattan office building, it seemed. I had heard weird things about this man who decided, when it pleased him, what New Yorkers would read with their morning coffee, but this was weirdness raised to a higher level.

He sat down in his chair again and was silent, until he leaned forward once more and pointed a bony finger at me.

'What story are you working on?' he asked

'Tammany.'

He arched his fingers together and nodded.

'He was an Indian,' he said.

He? Who?

'He was a sachem of a tribe of Delaware Indians called the Lenni-Lenape.'

If he was making this up, as I presumed he was, since Tammany was no more than the name of a bunch who had dedicated themselves to plundering New York for a hundred years or more, he was pretty fast with his crazy stories.

'Discovered corn, beans, and tobacco. Used tobacco to keep the fleas off.'

I smothered a laugh with a cough, or hoped I had.

'It was him that welcomed Penn and gave him the land, which is how come he came to be known as Saint Tammany of Philadelphia.'

All of which would have been further evidence for getting him carried away to somewhere secure where he could do no harm to anyone, except that later I looked it up and by God he was right. It turned out that in the War of Independence he was a patron saint of the army and we nearly ended up celebrating May 12th rather than the fourth of July, since that was his day. Even when the boys downtown began to get together to steal the coins off dead men's eyes and plunder anything they could get, they dressed up as Indians and called themselves braves and warriors. Apparently, Tammany came from Tamanend, a leader of a tribe called the Lenape. Even their leader was known as the Grand Sachem, that being a chief of the Algonquin. I remembered a cartoon by Thomas Nash in *Harper's* with a bunch of Indians dancing round a Tammany pole while scalping a woman who represented the country. At the time I didn't see the connection. I was glad to learn that the Saint himself wasn't quite so saintly, burning himself to death when drunk. But even so the members used to meet in what they called a wigwam. Faced with the old man pulling this out of the air, though, and knowing nothing about Tammany beyond Boss Tweed, Honest John Kelley and Richard Croker, I took this as further evidence of insanity.

He fell silent again. A log slipped forward, sending a cascade of red and orange onto the hearth. A spark or two fell on one of his pointed leather shoes and smouldered there. I didn't know whether to say anything or not. If I did it might imply he was too far gone to know when he was on fire. If I didn't what was I going to do, watch him go up in flames out of sheer politeness? In the end he waved his hand to me, which I took for a dismissal. In case I was wrong I got up real slowly so that he could correct my mistake. But he said nothing, and it wasn't until I was at the door and wondering whether I should say goodbye or not and, if so, what I should say ('Well, I've got to be going now.'

'See you around,' 'Regards to Mrs ...') when his face appeared once more, and he waved me on my way with a three-word blessing: 'A dollar each.'

I closed the door behind me, none too sure by now whether he was complaining at the price of buffalo hides or objecting to the expense of killing Indians. Either way I was out of there before he had burst into flames, and counted that a decided advantage as I descended the staircase to the world of printer's ink and cynicism on the other side of a frosted glass door.

As far as I knew there had just been the two occasions when he had invited someone up for these little talks, and I got to pull the short straw both times. For the most part he was content to send his messages in a vacuum tube so that the editor, who boasted to anyone who would see fit to listen that he was his own man and made his own decisions, would get to know just how he was to use his freedom in the next edition. How come I got to be granted the privilege heaven knows. I wasn't buying that guff about my writing. Maybe he regarded me as surplus to requirements and was sending me where I might get killed or scalped though, come to think of it, they go together.

I went straight to see Fickey, noticing in passing that the gold letters on his door were peeling off so that they declared "ROMULUS FICK ED ." Romulus? Why had I never noticed that before? And perhaps we were all ficked. Meanwhile, if he didn't already know about the job I had just been given he would get to hear soon enough anyway.

I didn't knock, taking pride in not doing so. There had come a first time when I nerved myself not to do so. He took no notice that I could see so that I was hardly sure which one of us had won, or even if there was a contest of any kind in the first place. He looked up at me, a pencil behind each ear and no fewer than three cups of coffee on the desk beside him, all half full, and a fifth of bourbon in the drawer, as I had reason to know.

'Indians!' he said, and he wasn't asking, either. He remembered the last time when they had all wasted time and money and he had had to spike everything I wrote.

'Yep. Something about it costing too much or too little to kill them off. And, apparently, they've taken to dancing if you're thinking of running a dance column.'

'When?'

'Not clear. Maybe we can hold it off until he's forgotten it.'

He reached for his drawer and took the bourbon out, two fingers thrust down into glasses that were dirty enough without ink and God knows what else besides.

'He never forgets,' was all he said, and I could see from the bourbon that he knew we were going to have to go along with whatever madness came from upstairs. 'You don't know the half,' he said, and splashed a little in each glass, rather more in his own, but it was his whisky we were drinking.

'Tell you something about him,' he said staring at me with those swimming blue eyes of his. 'He's halfway crazy.'

'Half way?'

'And some. You never knew his father.'

'No.'

'A prince.'

It didn't seem likely, not if the cuckoo in the attic was the best he could do.

'Founded the paper.'

I could see it was my day for history lessons though I would as soon have been out of there.

'Well, chief, got to be going. Got the Tammany story to do.'

'Tammany! Just you walk careful. Pick your targets.'

'Sure,' I said, knowing the limits of our crusading zeal. Under Honest John Kelly the *Star* and the *Evening Express* had both been Tammany papers. In fact, the Board of Excise Commissioners wouldn't give a saloon keeper a licence unless he could show paid-up receipts for two subscriptions to the *Star*. Which was how come we had started our campaign, but there are limits when Tammany controls just about everything, from the cop on the beat to the mayor in his mansion. Used to be there was a 'Dough Day' before elections when the dough was handed out to buy the votes.

'And forget the Indians. For now.' This from the man who had just got through telling me he never forgets.

And he wouldn't. That much I knew. Unless he was fully on fire by now or managed to smoulder away before it came time for me to pack my clothes.

'Sit down,' said who everyone called Mike but who I now needed to think of as some ancient Roman, glancing at the clock as if it made any kind of difference what time he set himself to start his drinking. 'Time for another dram.'

'Time enough,' I said, and sat down on a chair where generations of young reporters had squirmed as their prose was torn apart. He could strip a piece down to its essentials faster than Katy O'Rourke could perform the same function for the sailors at the Hell Hole.

'The Tammany piece,' he said.

'Yes,' I replied, interested in how he would go about it this time, telling me to steer clear of this man or that, to forget this little operation or that little scam. We were 'a progressive paper.' It said so on the masthead. It was just that you had to be careful where you progressed and at what speed.

'Mike, you have no need to say a thing.'

'Right,' he said, and slopped another drink in both glasses before I had had a chance to drink the first. He looked at his glass as though the mere sight of it put him into a reverie.

'Thing about a newspaper,' he began, and then lost his way as he looked at me through a glass misted with fingerprints and regret. So, I never heard what the thing about a newspaper was, anyway having my own ideas on that front. It was where I went to earn a dollar as other men turned up to clean the drains or drill someone's teeth. And the way I earned my dollar wasn't so different since I spent my time sifting through the muck and noting the decay. There were times I thought it was about telling people things they ought to know, but I was younger then. I also thought I would be

treading water until I published my novel, a fearless
exposure of fearless exposures, my hero, of course,
being a young reporter dedicated to Truth, Honesty and
all the things I had learned to skirt around if I was to
make it in a city that had illusions about itself and
wanted to hold onto them. I would be an Ibsen truth
teller, though come to think of it they didn't come off
too well. I'd taken to reading him whenever I felt
depressed just to see it was possible to be more
depressed but then, he is Scandinavian and it's dark
there for much of the year. Somehow the novel never
got written but then most of the newspaper men I knew
thought they would write a novel, meanwhile lowering
the value of their linguistic currency given that they
would be read by people who liked familiar words and
when it came to syllables couldn't get beyond two,
though with a preference for one. "Respect the reader,"
Mike had said when I first arrived, but even then I could
see he was trying not to smile.

CHAPTER FOUR: CROCKER

I took myself off where I always take myself
when I want to do some thinking. I went to the New
York and Brooklyn Bridge. I had watched it go up,
from those first loops of wire, hanging down like saliva
from the great buttresses, and then the roadbed edging
out across the East River. The granite blocks had come
down from Maine by schooner and some, I was told,
from Connecticut. It was designed by some German
who had his toes cut off and died. It was built as a
symbol, not just another way to get across the river, and
it was as a symbol that I responded. Hey, this was the
nineteenth century, already edging out toward the
twentieth telling us we could make it, though there were
those that said we couldn't.

As soon as it was finished, I was up there,
walking across, looking one way to Red Hook and the
other to Manhattan, two worlds that wanted nothing to
do with each other but had got linked together because
someone thought it a good idea. And somehow, when I
was up there, I was nowhere in particular and so could

get some thinking done. Whatever story I was on, whatever relationship was falling apart because the woman in question couldn't seem to square me with her own plans for domestic bliss and etc., this was where I would come to get away from it, looking down where already people had decided it was a good place to get rid of their problems altogether, jumping into the swirling water.

Come to think of it, it was amazing the bridge got to be built at all, what with everyone paying everyone off until there didn't seem too much left for the steel and rocks. But here it was, and it seemed pretty fine to me. And if we could do this, throw it up against the sky, well, who knew what might lie ahead. This was the right time to be born and this was the right place as well. You could feel the energy coming up from both sides of the river. I always left there feeling better than I arrived. I guess it was particular to me, though, because those who swung their legs over the side and dropped into the water below must have missed out on the energy part.

I'm not from here. That's what makes here here. I come from another place that wasn't anything, a no

place that people called home, except I didn't. It never
seemed that way to me. Your eyes could focus twenty
miles off and everyone thought God was around
somewhere, or everywhere. They could never quite
make their minds up which. There was a church where
they told you that hell awaited and sang songs about
salvation if only you would bend the knee. I was never
good at that. You wouldn't call it a town, the place I
lived. It had a name, but no one here would recognise it.
Who cares about a bunch of houses in amongst the
wheat where there are winds that will twist around and
lift cows and people and anything they've a mind to, a
place where the heat will shrivel the crops or snow
sweep down from the north until the cattle have to be
dug out? I guess they settled there because the wheels
fell off the wagon so that they never got where they
wanted and so stayed where they were, or because that
summer the rains had come so that it seemed a place to
stay, finding otherwise but too late to change their
minds.

When I decided to leave, I thought to go west.
We always go west. Except I got turned around and
chose to rebel even against the compass. One parent

dead, the other adrift in his mind, there was nothing to hold me, no duty I couldn't give up on. He would have understood except he didn't understand a thing. He had already gone somewhere himself and I couldn't go with him.

Born a year after Fort Sumpter fell, I arrived in violence. Barely a year later Quantrill raided Lawrence, less than a hundred miles away and named for an abolitionist. 180 dead. One of them was the outlaw Jesse James who died the day I arrived in New York, shot in the head by Robert Ford. Three months later, James Garfield was shot dead in Washington. Killing presidents could become a habit.

So here I am, twenty-eight, making my way up from office boy to whatever I now am. This is my city and I discovered that once you got to know it you found it wasn't as big as you thought. All the places that mattered came together in your mind and a lot of it you could walk, if you didn't mind taking your life in your hands, sweating beyond belief in summer and turned to ice in the winter. But where to go from here? Not to Washington for sure, though already I had been asked. Who would want to go to a pork barrel stuck out in a swamp? Politicians were dirt on any level, but these didn't even care. At least Tammany thought it made sense to get the ward bosses out to fires, weddings, and funerals. At least they spread their money around a little. Not far, of course, and spread pretty thin, but they knew that every now and then they would be needing votes and though they could stuff ballots and buy what they needed, still there was something in them liked to think that people had actually gone in to put their cross because they appreciated what you did when you weren't swindling everyone and easing opponents into the river where a man had lost his toes, bodies having lost selective parts each one a message if you understood the language.

The Indians didn't bother me. Either the whole thing would go away, and then who was to worry, or I would get to go on another chase and come back with nothing but get paid just the same, and see a bit more of the country than I could even from up here on the top of the world, on the top of my world at least. Right now, though, I had a thing or two to do. And the first was catch a train to Hartford to hear what an insurance director had to say, except that this insurance director was a millionaire by the name of Mark Twain.

Well, not quite the first. First, I had to go to Houlihan's, its floor covered with sawdust to soak up the beer and the sweat and, after a certain time of night, the blood. I am not Irish myself, except when it comes to drinking, but most of those who came to Houlihan's were reporters like me, accepted as honorary Micks. It draws people like a magnet. Round about ten or eleven the arguments would start. Faces would turn red, muscles bulge, veins stand out like rivers in red sand, and those blue eyes would lose their focus. Then fists and knees and chairs and anything not screwed down would be swung and for ten minutes or so it was best to be under a table, before the cops strolled in and laid a few out with their clubs. Then it was all fine again and the cops stayed on for a drink or two and Houlihan's was back to what it was best as, a place to meet and talk and get things done that couldn't be done at other times and other places.

I was there to meet Paddy Callaghan who had an obscure job in City Hall and, for a few dollars every now and then, would slip me pieces of information, sometimes trivial, sometimes pointing me in the right direction, though I never told him that or he would think he mattered. He was a man who liked to believe he was a secret agent of some kind, though no secret agent would choose to meet in Houlihan's. I saw him come in, collar turned up, eyes flicking from one side of the room to the other. I leaned out of the booth so he could see me, which he did though Houlihan's preferred to keep the lights down low so people couldn't see what they were eating and drinking, this not being a place known for its food, at least not in a good sense.

He slid himself in and I passed him a glass. It was part of the ritual, as a baby has water sprinkled on it as a warning that that's how life will be with people dumping on you when there is nothing you can do about it.

'Mr Smythe,' he said, nodding for me to pour. 'How's yourself?'

'I'm fine, Mr Callaghan. And how is City Hall?' Smythe seemed to me a step above Smith when it came to fake names.

He raised a finger to his lips and ducked his head down as if the mere mention of City Hall was enough to bring the authorities down on him. Then he leaned forward, a hand clapped theatrically to his mouth.

'There's things there you wouldn't credit.'

There was very little I wouldn't credit, having worked this beat for a couple of years, but also very little I was ready to credit if it came only from his lips.

'The money,' he said.

'The money.'

'Like there was no tomorrow.'

He had a way of speaking elliptically that required a deal of patience if you were to make any sense of it. And he had a fondness for clichés. They were somewhere he could go when language proved a challenge. I had half the story already. The City Treasurer was syphoning money directly into Tammany pockets, hardly news to the citizenry at large. The real story was what they had done to stop the news getting out. The real news was a body found in the Battery with three fingers missing and one eye put out, and not some derelict that had wandered into their path but an official of a bank through whose accounts the money had passed. The Battery was formed from landfill, so perhaps they thought it was a good place to dump human refuse.

'Papers,' I said, 'evidence, people prepared to go on the record. You've given me nothing I can use.'

'Patience,' he says, 'I have to take care, or I'll be joining you know who.'

I poured him another. I had few hopes, to tell the truth. He was good for the small stuff, the small change of corruption you could jingle in your pocket. I doubted he was good for anything more. But a whisky or two was a small enough price to pay, especially given the quality of whisky in Houlihan's, cheap by virtue of a not always discrete infusion of water. If you wanted the good stuff you needed to pay extra when you ordered.

There was a smell to Houlihan's that would enable a blind man to find it from half a mile off. It was the beer and the whisky alright, but along with that went the stink of sweat, honest and otherwise, along with a particularly awful cologne the owner chose to drown

69

himself in, believing it to make him attractive to the women who almost never ventured into the bar, those that did smelling much the same as him. It was where we hacks came from time to time -- there being no lack of choice in that part of town -- but also those who yearned for the Ireland they had been so glad to leave. The sound of a fiddle would set them off or some sickly song about a young woman called Kitty, or one county or other, each of which they made sound like heaven on earth, which made you wonder why they chose to settle in Harlem along with the Italians and the Jews. Oh, New York was the place to come all right, bringing with you this and that, throwing it in the common pot until out came a New Yorker who would as soon spit in your eye as wish you the time of day.

'It would help if I had a little money to be going on with.'

'Money is for results, and I know how you would be going on with it if you had it,' I said, pouring him another drink just the same, for in my experience the more liquor he consumed the more information he would offer up. But instead of that the tears began to come into his eyes and rather than face the story of his terrible upbringing in County Cork or County Wicklow or Dublin or wherever it was he claimed as home, I decided to leave him there, with what remained of the bottle, which I would put down as expenses when the story eventually hit the paper.

'Tell me, I said, 'what do you know about Indians and Saint Tammany,'

He looked at me as if I were just off the boat, as well he might.

'Forget it.'

'Who are these Indians, Mr Smythe?'

I don't know why I asked him. 'Forget it. Tell me, how much would it cost if a man wanted to be a patrolman?'

'A regular patrolman?'

'Yes.'

'It would depend, but three hundred dollars would do it. But they get it back from the prostitutes.'

'And a Captain?'

'Well, a Captain, now that's something else again. That would cost you a deal, what with what you could hope to make on it. Five thousand, ten thousand, maybe more. Depends on the district.'

'Can a man really make enough back to justify the likes of that?'

'And why not? Take Clubber Williams.'

'Here in the Tenderloin.'

'The very same. And how do you think it came to be called that, Mr Smythe? When he was transferred from the precinct he was in he said he had taken enough from the rump and that now it was time for him to have a taste of the tenderloin. Saloons pay $20, then there are the pool rooms, policy shops.'

The Tenderloin, between Fourteenth Street and Forty-Second Street, between Fourth and Seventh Avenue, was where we were. And Clubber Williams had earned his name in the very way you would think, subtlety not being his strong suit even if he had known the word.

'Tell the truth, Mr Smythe, I shouldn't be seen with you here. You are known, you see.'

'So are you, I dare say. Next time, then.'

'Next time, Mr Smythe. And the money?'

'There is no money. Not until you've got something more definite to say.'

He slid out of the booth, where we had been partially hidden, looking around as he did. And he was right to do so. There wasn't one of the Tammany crowd who would hesitate to bust your head, and worse. They didn't even need to be paid. Some did it as a hobby, which was more enjoyable than baseball but, then, what isn't. Croker himself had been up for murder and before that had been a street fighter ready to beat all others. I waited a few minutes and then followed.

I noticed them straight away. They were leaning on the bar, staring straight at me, and when I moved toward the door, they left their glasses half full. Nobody did that in Houlihan's. They set out toward me, not looking right, or left, ready to elbow anyone got in their way, not that anyone would. You didn't need to be introduced to know what they were about.

I tried to make it look as if I hadn't seen them, but how do you do that? I pushed the door open and stepped into the rain. There was a streetlamp directly outside, casting a pool of light around it, turning the rain into slivers of steel. There was no one else in sight. Most had probably made their way into bars much as I had done, or gone home to wives who kept a time clock on them. I looked for a cab but there were none around, except one, already occupied, going away from me in a spin of water, the spray from the wheels caught by another light further off like a cascade of gold coins I stood for a moment, unsure whether I was better off trying to get home or stepping back inside where there were enough people to maybe stop them doing what they had a mind to do. Then again, I told myself, perhaps I had simply got too sensitive. What did I have to worry about? I had met someone, talked to someone, and now was going home. Nothing had passed. I was none the wiser now than I had been before. In fact, I did step back inside, only to see them no more than half a dozen paces away and looking straight at me. I stepped

back out. The cab was still just in sight, and I thought
that maybe another would be along any moment. There
were times when you couldn't move for cabs. This
wasn't one of them. I set off to follow it but heard the
rush of noise as the door opened and closed behind me.

I wouldn't be the first reporter to have had a few
bones broken to help him write more to the point. I
quickened my pace, trying not to run, as if that would
make any difference. I wrote for a living. I didn't run
for it. There were half a dozen blocks before I would
come to my building, and then there was no guarantee
they wouldn't put their boots through the door and then
through me. I considered the other possibilities,
walking as fast as I dared convinced that if I did run it
would somehow precipitate what I knew was going to
happen anyway.

The rain came on heavier suddenly and found its
way straight through the coat that clung coldly to me.
The two behind didn't have coats. Perhaps they would
leave it for another day. Except that they didn't,
because I chanced a glance behind and saw them
coming on as if rain meant no more to them than

anything else, a couple of arrows on their way to a target.

There was a hotel just two blocks further on. I could see a glow of light from its entrance. I pulled my collar tight around my neck, as the water streamed down, and leant into the wind, which was getting up now so that the rain seemed to come horizontally. But those are long blocks around there and seemed longer now than they had in the past. And where were the police? Well, that was a joke. If these were Tammany, and who else might they be, the police were paid to keep well away and perhaps it was as well they did because they might have taken over to save their friends from getting wet.

I was up to my ankles in water as I crossed at the intersection and had barely reached the other side of the street when I heard them behind, even over the shushing of the rain. There was the thud of their feet. I decided this was a good time to forget what I had told myself about not running and set in to sprint as fast as I could. But, heavy though they looked, I was slowed by liquor and cigarettes no doubt, and knew right away I wasn't going to make it.

He spun me round and pushed me back against the wall. I could smell the liquor on his breath. I tried to resist but the other man caught hold of my wrists. Evidently liquor didn't slow them at all but, then, this was what they did. They had Ireland printed across their foreheads, one wearing a round hat, too small for him, which made him look something of a clown, though I decided against telling him as much. He had a chubby, almost baby-like face, but since he was several inches taller than me and had muscles that his ill-fitting clothes did nothing to conceal, I wasn't about to remark on that either. The other man, his dark hair slicked down by the rain, had a sharp nose and eyes that darted around as if someone might rescue me, as no one would even had the street been full of people. Some things it was better to ignore. The distant hotel was no less distant now, its light mocking my attempts to reach it.

'Got a message for you?' said the tall one grinding his fist into my shoulder. 'Do you hear me, got a message for you.'

I did hear, oh, yes, I heard all right.

'You hear?'

'Yes,' I said. Maybe that was all it was. Maybe they would be content to tell me to look in someone else's trash can, whistle some other tune. Maybe, only I doubted it. The rain was going down my neck now and I could feel it trickle cold across my chest.

Then his face went blank, and it was evident that he couldn't remember his message word for word, as he had doubtless been instructed to deliver it.

'You been … I'm to say …'

This might have gone on for some time had his companion, who evidently had a better memory or less patience, leaned forward and hissed in my ear.

'Stop asking questions.'

There was a moment's silence during which it was obvious that the first man somewhat resented having his role appropriated and was still struggling to recall his message in its entirety.

'What questions?' I was stupid enough to ask.

The two looked at each other, as if unsure that this didn't take them somewhat beyond their remit. Evidently my role was to crumple on the spot, perhaps plead a little, beg. None of these options were entirely out of my mind but, for the moment, I thought I would play things along in case a cab came by, or people, or the world ended.

Then the thin faced one, who evidently had cunning if not intelligence, hissed again: 'Any.'

'Look, lads' I said, affecting a deal more calmness than I felt, 'you've delivered your message. But you must tell those that sent you that they've got the wrong man.'

They looked uneasily at each other. I could see they were taking what I'd said entirely literally, despite having seen me with an informer, if they realised that was who it was, as perhaps they did not.

'No, sir, that we've not.'

It was a curious locution and I almost lost track of what I was going to say, always assuming that I knew what that was as now I am not so sure. Where did the 'sir' come from, unless they were capable of rising to irony, which, as you will gather, I doubted?

'You have got the wrong man because, like you, I am only doing what I am told. You have your bosses; I have mine. You have done your job; I do mine. The man they want is in the *Telegraph* building and my betting is that your bosses and he can sort all these things out.'

There was another pause and somewhere in the distance I could hear the steady clip clop of a horse's hooves.

'Should I hit him one, Mike?' said the big man, evidently recalling the way these things are normally conducted.

It was not a question whose answer I was anxious to hear, so I pulled away, suddenly, stepping into the light from a streetlamp as the cab drew nearer.

'Just tell him that,' I said, and stepped ankle deep into the water flooding along the street as I held up my hand and the cab driver gave his horse a flick and pulled over toward me. A miracle!

I stepped up before either one of them had thought of the best way to handle this and we were on our way when the big man put a foot into the gutter as if to take hold of the cab. In doing so, however, he, too, found himself up to the ankle in water and was sufficiently disturbed to step away, so that we were gone. The other one shouted something after me but what with the wind and the rain, the sound of the horse's hooves and the gritty rush of wheels on the road, I couldn't hear what it was he said. I gave the man my address, wondering as I did so on the wisdom of it, since maybe he would sell it on to those who wished to follow me. But then I realised that of course my address was hardly difficult to come by and that they could drop by whenever they had a mind to do so.

Back in my apartment I lit a fire and stripped off. I sat as close as I could to get the warmth back into my bones and rubbed myself down with a towel which even I had to admit could have done with a wash a week or two before. I slipped into some dry clothes, poured myself a stiffer drink than even I am used to doing, and sat beside my pants and shirt as they steamed gently in the flickering light.

Every now and then in my job you were forced to ask yourself how far you were willing to go. Life is a

matter of compromise, I am inclined to believe. It is all
very well for some to have principles, and I have them
myself from time to time, but there are moments when
principles come up against survival. To tell the truth I
had been threatened before and by more accomplished
thugs than these. I had also been roughed up a little,
though unlike others of my trade had no broken bones to
show for it. The fact is that if you wanted to get
anywhere you had to come up with the goods and that
meant exclusives, which meant discovering things that
others couldn't or wouldn't or felt it best not to know.
As warnings go this was pretty friendly. If whoever
sent them had been serious, they would have picked
someone who could remember what it was they were
supposed to say and do so for longer than it took to walk
down the street and go into a bar.

And I had reason to know they could be more
inventive. When I first started out, and was living in a
single room in a walk-up on 12th Street, I had crossed a
man who had a line in violence I thought people should
know about. He disagreed. One day I began to smell
something I assumed must be a dead rat and sure
enough, less than a week later, flies began to beat

against the window, not one or two but twenty and thirty at a time. I tried the landlord, but rats were like pet cats around there, something you were supposed to accept when they moved in. 'It's the heat,' he said, which, given it only came on a couple of hours a day with a noise like someone hitting the pipes with a wrench, seemed unlikely. In the end I called in a favour from a man whose name I had kept out of a story. He told me he'd see to it while I was out, which suited me fine because the smell had become worse so that my breakfast bagel tasted like shit. When I came back there were cops everywhere. He had taken the floorboards up and instead of a rat found a body, which put me in a hole, or would have done but for the fact that the man who had broken in and laid this particular egg in my nest had also left a note in the corpse's pocket threatening to kill him and even signed it. But then he was known for his fists rather than his brain. You had to grant him an imagination, though. I had once done something similar with a fish under a teacher's desk, at the time thinking it well worth the thrashing I got as a result.

83

I spent a day at the precinct, but it didn't take them long to figure out what had happened. I even saw them bring him in. His defence turned out to be that the man was dead when he put him there. I said he wasn't too bright. I couldn't go back to my room, though. The stink wouldn't go away. But that's New York. It never does.

Meanwhile, what of my informant? If they knew about me, they knew about him. And if they felt some scruple about me – and it seemed they did or they would have sent more professional bailiffs to dispossess me of my opinions – they would feel nothing for him. And even if he was no better than them, and I was secure on that score, nonetheless I wouldn't fancy seeing him in the morgue staring up at me. But what was to be done? Well, what was to be done was forget it all or, better yet, find some other route to the truth buried somewhere not so far away. Besides, there was little I could do for him. I had no idea of his address and could hardly walk into City Hall to give him a warning, though I resolved to get a note to him somehow. But tomorrow was tomorrow, though perhaps those who went after me had more than one job to do. Maybe that was why the gentle giant, whose fist had bored its way into my shoulder so that it was already blooming red and blue, had forgotten what message he was supposed to be delivering.

Nor did I expect much sympathy if I told people what had happened. There was certainly no point in putting anything in the paper. REPORTER TOLD NOT TO ASK QUESTIONS was not exactly the kind of headline that would shock people at their breakfast tables. No blood, no broken bones, two anonymous men. And when it came to public sympathy newspapermen ranked even lower than politicians, amazing though that seemed. What was wrong with what we did? We cleaned the stables. We didn't put the shit there in the first place. But there you are, I never took this job on to be loved by anyone and if I had it would have been a major disaster since love was what I had never had from any source as far as I could tell.

I banked the fire up, moved the clothes further away from it, and went to bed, with a final glass to settle myself. I had been there no more than ten minutes and was just drifting off when there came a tap at my door, not the kind of tap that a couple of Tammany boys would give. But I was expecting no one. Nonetheless, I did what I should not have done. I got up, pulled my pants on, and opened the door.

Outside was a bedraggled girl, black paint smeared down from her eyes, her face pale in the lamplight.

'Please, sir,' she said 'I was told to come here. And I was to say I was already paid for.'

Subtlety had never been their strength. It almost made me laugh, except that I felt insulted they thought I could be bought off so easily. I had seen a deal of this side of their work, having run a story that took me into the dark tenements where men and women did what they had to in order to survive another day. Those that owned them kept the money, passing on some to those that let the whole thing thrive. There were places where police would be on hand in case of trouble. But it wasn't the girls they were there to protect.

'Go home,' I said. 'You've got the wrong address.' One moment threat, the next bribe.

She looked terrified, so I added, 'not the wrong address, just the wrong person. Tell them what you like but be on your way.' Still she just stood there, not knowing what to do, as doubtless she did not, living in fear of what might be done. And why was she there? Was she a simple bribe or was she supposed to leave the door unlocked so they could pile on in and finish the job? I was not tempted. There might have been times when I would have been, and perhaps if they had chosen someone other than this poor girl, broken and bruised, wet through. But, no, I am beyond that and anyway insulted that they could think so simple a trap could be sprung. Either way, I closed the door on that smudged face. I locked it again, making double sure this time.

I wasn't paid so much that I fancied this kind of life running away from people who couldn't spell their own names. I made my way back to bed, as doubtless she did to hers, but I chose not to think where that might be as I took one more glass before drifting off to sleep. It was the final glass that gave me the dreams, even if it was the two charmers from Houlihan's who furnished the cast of the drama in which I played before waking in the morning to a bright blue sky and air so fresh that it purged all memories of the dream and took the sting out of an encounter on a rainy New York street.

And what do you know, two days later I got a call from the morgue, and it was even as I had thought it would be. Biblical. Fished out of the river so that, at first, they put him down as a drunk. Then they found where the knife had gone in, under the left arm, long and thin and deadly so that he wouldn't be going to Houlihan's again. And I must admit it got me to more than thinking. It got me to throwing up, which was what I didn't do in all the years I had been at the morgue.

'Is it the smell?' asked the assistant, who didn't know me too well but was just someone I slipped a ten to on a regular basis.

'The smell?' I said, when I had recovered enough to be chatty. 'No, it isn't the smell. It's the thought that somebody did that just because somebody else told them to.'

'All the time.' he said.

'What?'

'Like him. All the time. Not many, but regular.'

'Yes,' I said, kind of flat, because in my mind I was seeing myself there. I was used to the other kind, the kind that ended up here because they had no money and did things that disgusted them, eventually, so that they took the jump from my bridge, or simply slipped into the water and did nothing to stop themselves drifting to the bottom. I supposed I was used to this kind, too. But certainly, there was no shortage of those I had looked at with neat little black holes in them or sometimes half their heads gone.

And then I thought, what of the girl I had sent away? What had they done to her when they found she hadn't done whatever it was she was supposed to have done? Unless it was just a bribe, in which case I dare say she could lie her way out of it. Just the same I looked at all the bodies lying there. She wasn't among them, but that didn't mean a thing. Besides, there were other ways of killing people than hitting them over the head or dropping them in the river.

When I started out this was one of the places I was sent on a regular basis, here and the police

departments to see what was on the blotter. For a while
we got frozen out of that because of Tammany but
eventually they lost interest or figured it wasn't worth
the effort since I could move around the city as fast as
anyone and even they found it hard to square everyone
off about us.

Sometimes it was the police that did it. They
simply took someone out in an alley and finished it
there rather than have the trouble of running the whole
thing through the courts. Other times they looked the
other way or, as I found after a time, kept guard at the
end of a street so that others could do what they had
been told without even knowing why it was being done.
These were not good times in New York. There were
people here who did not care, simply did not care what
they did. And when there's a situation like that the
crazies come to the top like froth on a beer. And if they
turn out a liability well, they, too, could end up on a slab
in the ice room at the morgue, not thinking, I suppose,
that this could be so even though that was the business
they were in.

Maybe it was a result of immigration. What was
there to do when you came off the boat? You got taken

in, not knowing anything, just doing what someone told you to. Even so, it didn't make sense that people could be turned around. Why did they come? Because they had hope. And how do you get to keep hope alive when what you are told to do is shoot someone in the head or even just break their kneecaps because they didn't pay what they were told they owed, not owing because it was a legitimate debt but because they ran a crap game or an envelope game or the policies. There were a hundred ways of making a living out there, most of them illegal and perhaps not doing all that much harm. But every one of them carried a tax and your job was to see they paid it on a regular basis, and to remind them if they didn't. But was this why they left their homes in Palermo or Donegal or somewhere in the back end of Europe? And what did they tell their wives when they went out to work and what did they tell them when they came home with blood on their clothes? This was America. This was the place they had given everything up to come to, and this is where they were scared now to walk down the street, scared even to open the door in case there was someone there with a baseball bat, and not to invite you to a game, either. Or maybe a pistol and a smile on their faces.

Most got by, managed to edge their way upward, put a little aside, even though they were paying people off, so that soon someone else was on the firing line, was the first to get the bat in the face. And if you played with the system rather than against it who knows, one day you might get to hold the bat yourself, to drag some guy into a corner and talk to him about his family and the need to be part of another family. Maybe one day you got to edge him into the river, wish him on his way to eternity. The morgue was the end of a thousand stories. They had started somewhere with green hills and a thousand years of history. They had started maybe from hunger and persecution, since America didn't invent either one of them, but they came with an idea that went wrong. Not for all of them, of course. It was easy to get bitter simply because you were a reporter and saw things most people didn't.

Stop the rich, if you dare, the rich who live around Washington Square, and ask them if this isn't paradise on earth and they would look at you as if you were crazy. Of course, it is paradise. Look at their houses, look at the neighbourhood. Look at the carriages. They were the people turned money into culture, draped their homes with art, went to the bank on a regular basis. They never went to the morgue. They were lucky. They never even got burned by thieves. They paid their dues just the same, put money in the pockets of those who promised to keep them separate from that other side, most probably never realising who it was were getting paid. They never asked how much was added on in stores or bars or clubs to keep the system going. As far as they were concerned America was the acme of civilisation and they the acme of America. They couldn't wait for the new century to come because they knew it would belong to them. Europe was the place people left, somewhere to visit, a museum to look after history, to give them the culture they buried themselves in. What would they think, if they had been brought down here and shown the underside? I know what they would have thought. We need more cops, we need tougher magistrates, we need someone to sweep all this away and if not away then somewhere they would never have to look at it.

93

He slid the body back in the wall of lockers as if this were a store and the corpses so many samples ready to be displayed.

'Know him?' he asked.

'Not really,' I said, knowing that if I paid him to let me look then someone else paid him to say who I had been looking at.

'Anything else?' I asked, more to cover myself than anything.

'Just a couple of girls got cut up in one of the cat houses. Cut each other up, I dare say. Sometimes I think they're not human, these people. Doing that.'

This was the time when whisky cost ten cents a pint and you could buy a girl for not much more than the price of a bottle. How do you stay human in the middle of that? How do you cling onto yourself when everything you did and everything everyone else did told you you were nothing? Likely thing was that they had been cut up by a customer or if not that then by those that kept them there. And those were the people on my track. It didn't make me feel good in there. I had always thought New York was my town but I guess I had come to feel that I had had my fill. And now there were those telling me much the same.

This was not the first time I had got tangled up with Croker. I got an invitation, if you could call three men coming up to me on the street and instructing me where to go, an invitation. It seemed I was to meet Richard Croker himself. Here I had been, as per usual, with no evidence at all, merely sniffing round the edges of a stink on the sidewalk and suddenly I was promoted house guest of Tammany's leader. What it told me then, of course, was that I was onto something, that or he wanted some favour that only I could do, which seemed unlikely but, then, everything was unlikely where he was concerned.

Years back he had been the leader of the Fourth Avenue Tunnel Gang in which capacity he had bitten a man's ear off and fought Dick Lynch, a prize fighter, knocking all his teeth out and damaging him in ways that were still spoken of. Only man ever beat him was 'Ed' Quigley and he was found one day in the tunnel with both legs cut off by a train. People did not mess with the Boss of New York, even if too many lunches and too much booze had slowed him down a bit. Back in '74 he'd shot a man on election day and been put on trial for murder. After seventeen hours the jury couldn't make up its mind, so he went free. I'm not saying he fired the shot, but he fired the shot.

He sat in a swivel chair, much like a barber's. At first, he paid no attention to me but went on talking to two cronies who leaned toward him as if he were a priest and they were making confession, which perhaps they were. Then he swung around and looked at me. I returned the compliment. He was forty-seven, or thereabouts, not publishing details about himself of this kind, though we were supposed to put them in our reports. Most reporters knocked half a dozen years off just to be safe, so that they didn't have parts of themselves knocked off in return. He had the Irish look about him red, splotchy face, pale blue eyes, sandy hair. He put out a stubby finger and beckoned me forward. Then the finger pointed at a chair as if I were hardly worth the effort of expending language. I sat down.

'Give the man a drink,' he said.

It was ten in the morning, but it didn't seem right to refuse. One of those who had picked me up brought a bottle across from another table and put it down in front of me along with a glass I would rather not have drunk out of since it was smeared with something best not enquired into.

He then waved the back of his hand and the same men melted away, if three people as heavy as they could be said to melt at all.

'I hear you want to talk to me.'

An interview? Why would I want to talk to him? I could think of nothing to say. I had written a piece or two, nothing you would think would get me noticed, but around here, it seemed, everything got you noticed. I wondered how many other reporters had been brought in here to get the treatment, be warned off, find something healthier to file their reports on.

'Always glad to oblige the press.'

I took a drink, feeling decidedly unprepared for this and remembering a couple of men who had been dogging my steps. Besides, maybe he was offering the drink to deaden the pain, the pain those who brought me in would doubtlessly be inflicting soon.

'Did you send a couple of bruisers after me last night, Mr Croker.' I asked, having had the treatment that time, too, and figuring it was best to get to the point, and better still to get out of there while I could. There were many who would have given a lot to have the chance I had, or thought they would, but there were many who hadn't had thugs sent after them and who anyway might have been changing their minds as I was tempted to maybe change mine. I was no crusader, after all. What did I care who robbed who of what? One story was as good as another from where I stood. If the cops didn't care, or the judges, or the magistrates, or anyone in this damn town then why should I? It worked, that was all they cared. It was growing fast and if it slid along on pig's grease, well, was there another kind?

He learned forward and out came that finger again, as if it were a blunt instrument, as, if rumours were correct, it was since 'Ed' Quigly had been short one eye as well as two legs when they found him, still alive, if you could call it that.

'I hope you're not wasting my time,' he said in a low voice full of cigars and Irish whisky.

Well, what was to be lost, except maybe various parts of myself in the Fourth Street tunnel.

'Do you believe in democracy?' I asked, aware straight away how stupid that would sound as if I were a sixth-grade school kid.

'Democracy, is it?' he said. 'Sure. In '64 I voted seventeen times. If a man is worth voting for once he is worth voting for seventeen times, wouldn't you say? Is a good man less good just because not enough people choose to vote for him?'

'And what did you think of Mr Tweed?'

Tweed had milked the city cow for everything it had until the poor animal collapsed and died. He had been thrown from office and Croker, who worked in the Comptroller's office under 'Slippery Dick' Connolly, got the push along with him. There was a reason people had the names they were given.

99

'I was amazed to hear what he had been doing. It's all a matter of record. So I worked for Honest John? So what?'

That he had, but before that he had worked for Tweed. It was he who took on a Republican politician and beat him so hard he never got back to work. And when Honest John, so called out of a sense of irony, he having also taken the city for all he could, made him Coroner of New York, he had been arrested for murder, which even Honest John must have felt was taking things a bit too far, though he got him out on bail.

As I say, he got off when the jury split. This was the man who was running New York and who I was debating the finer points of democracy with. Within a year or so he was Fire Commissioner, someone evidently having a sense of humour since it was rumoured he had been responsible for burning more than one bar that didn't pay its dues. As for Honest John Kelly (as opposed to alderman Honest John O'Neill, who got sentenced to four years in jail, the word 'Honest' clearly being something of a stretch), he was challenged by three-time Mayor Havemeyer, who was at odds with Tammany and unaccountably dropped dead of a stroke, it was said, a stroke of luck for Honest John who was in process of suing him for libel. He died the day of the trial. Nobody was surprised any more than they were when Honest John himself died having developed a habit of taking drugs to sleep, these proving terminally effective.

'It's true, isn't it that Mayor Grant appointed you City Chamberlain?'

'Maybe.'

'Worth $25,000 a year.'

'Public record.'

'And did you ever try to get him appointed Commissioner of Public Works?'

'And if I did?'

'By bribing the Board of Alderman?'

'Bribing? Bribing?'

'I heard $180,000.'

'Then you heard wrong.'

He was getting agitated now, and so was I, truth to tell.

'I hear tell it was all in dollar bills, in a satchel.'

He leaned forward, eyes narrowing.

'You want your legs broke?'

It wasn't what you looked to hear from a public official.

'I heard wrong?'

'You don't hear at all I hear one more word.'

I sat silently for a minute and then thought, what the hell. How many legs did I have to break?

'The way I heard it there's a cement works up in the Catskills and it's not called Rip Van Winkle, either.'

That last was sheer bravado because I could see from his face he didn't know what I was talking about, not about Rip Van Winkle anyway. 'Story was someone was going to get ten cents a barrel. Any comment?'

'You don't hear good, do you?'

His grammar was lousy, but he wasn't paid for that, though heaven knows what he was paid for exactly. Then, when I was getting ready for the sledgehammers to come out, he leant back in his chair and knitted his fingers together. Then he says,

'It was for Flossie.'

'Flossie? A cat?'

He leaned forward suddenly and hissed, 'Flossie's my daughter. He give her a present.'

'Who did?'

'Him you mentioned.'

'Grant?'

'When he was Sheriff.'

'How old is Flossie?'

'You don't mention Flossie.'

'How old is … your daughter.'

'Six or seven. I disremembers.'

'How much was she … paid?'

'Look, I taken all I'll take. Had you brung here because I thought maybe that would be the best. Now I see it ain't. Now I see you just some prick wants to make yourself a name. Well, you can make your name. And not how you'd like.'

I didn't know what to say. Most of the time they tried to pretend they were natural democrats, the people's friends. Nobody who didn't believe in democracy would bother to stuff the ballots. Some of the time they behaved as if they were aristocrats, believing money would buy them class, picking up property like the rest of the nouveau riche, tripping off to Newport, or if not Newport then Saratoga Springs or some of the less fashionable places in New York state. But love of money was the main thing. Respectability was neither here nor there. Knowing they could buy it, in the end they despised it. They needed the press because they wanted to be left alone and, if that sounds odd, they figured the best way to be left alone was to be seen as a kind of royalty, unapproachable, distant, in power by a kind of natural right that the rest of us only had to assent to. I guess that was why he called me in, but now he had evidently decided it wasn't such a great idea. The Fossett Committee had begun investigating corruption and who knew what they would turn up.

I don't remember how I got out of there. Half the time he was being the mayor, the other half he was planning how to lay me out across the railroad lines so that both legs would go at the same time. I asked him some more questions and his eyes got narrower and narrower until they were almost closed. Finally, he shut them and waved the back of his hand in my direction. A moment later a guiding hand threatened to break my wrist in two and I was ushered out and propelled into the street. Interview over.

I wrote it up with some care. There are ways of making a denial sound like a confession if you tried. I printed all his denials until there was a wall of them that seemed like one big admission. I was proud of it until a reporter I knew asked about my whitewash and I realised, what I hadn't before, that the reservations you keep in your head, and that create the irony you are trying for, are invisible to anyone else. All they get is what they read, and the irony stays where it was all the time. And talking of time, what should I get the next day, after my piece appeared and I had walked round proud of myself, but a gold watch, or gold looking at least, with a note saying that he had been pleased with what I had written. So, there you were. My contribution to keeping New York clean.

New York was the colour it was and had always been and nothing I did was going to smarten it up. It glittered gold, too, but I could be pretty sure that like my watch if I left it out in the rain it would turn another colour soon enough. Nothing was what it seemed in New York. Some loved it for that. Me, too, in some ways, I suppose. It gleamed but was as dirty as you please. And the smell of flowers was gone by noon so that all you were left with was the stench of money which to some, anyway, was the best smell of all.

Back in the office I got a look from Mike, who knew what had happened, as I guess, and when I went in there he says to me, 'So you got the treatment.'

'What treatment?'

'You got to meet the man.'

'Croker. Yes, of course. You read the piece.'

'Sure. Of course I read the piece. You did him a favour it seems to me.'

'A favour? I got all the charges there in print.'

'So you did. And all the denials, too. You going to get to him you gotta take another route. A straight line won't do it. That's for joining two places together by the shortest route. That's not the way you're going to make sense of what's out there. They're crooked; you got to be crooked, too, and I don't mean on the take. I mean, look for an angle. You got no angle here. All straight on. That won't never do.'

Now Crocker was off in Europe. Something to do with his health. In Wiesbaden, I had heard, taking the waters. It was because of the Fossett Investigation, no doubt, since there was water enough in this country. This had been going on for several weeks and they had been just as interested as me in Flossie and bags of money. But the fact that he was in Europe didn't mean that he didn't have an army to go about things in the normal way. Hence my visitors. The problem was that it wasn't so clear anymore who you could get to call them off.

There were advantages in Tammany that even I could see if you wanted someone you could talk to, to get things done. If you had a boy with no job, you just went along and they would see to it that he was signed onto somebody's books and it didn't matter whether he was needed or not, even whether he actually did a job. Need a few dollars to get by? They would oblige and not talk politics at you, either. They knew that politics was never about issues, but obligations. And these were people who knew about obligations. That much had survived from the old country. Someone did something for you, you repaid the debt. Someone did something against you, you repaid that as well. It was hard to see how you could break a power like that, especially when the other kind of politics was as rotten as anything Tammany ever thought up. It cloaked itself in another language but, at times at least, it came down to much the same thing.

CHAPTER FIVE: WHILE I LIVE, I HOPE

Happily, I had other stories to follow. I formed a temporary alliance, I guess you would call it, with a man who called himself a private detective. Anyone could call themselves that. A notice on the door was judged sufficient. He had been a cop and left for some reason he would never explain. I got involved because we were looking for the same person and I had the edge on him because I had one more arm than him and, truth to tell, one more eye. He never explained that either, though he obviously hadn't been that way when he was working in a precinct. They preferred whole people, damaged only by their fondness for dollars that would make them look away when it served their purpose. You will gather I am no friend of cops, nor they of me. I have been roughed up more than once, mistaken identity, they said, unable to suppress their smiles.

It was the eighteen-year-old daughter of a rich couple who lived in one of those apartments that go on for ever at the top of the Park. She had gone missing, and the cops had failed to do anything despite being

leaned on by everyone from the mayor down. The
Pinkertons had come up short, and they must have
worked a long way down the list to have ended up with
a man who seemed to have lost parts of himself and who
might therefore not be the best person to look for
someone whose whole body was missing. My guess is
that they had a host of other people looking, and not just
him. I met him when I was trying to find a man who had
worked in the finance department at City Hall and
figured nobody would miss the odd thousand given that
there were bigger thieves than him. Turned out they did,
though not enough to pay the bigger agencies to track
him down. Discrete, he said to me, finger to his nose.
At least he still had that.

It made a good story, but good stories are better
if they have an end. I met him in a bar. Where else do
we look if we're stuck on something. He needed the
publicity, and I needed a man, dead or alive, with
suitcases of cash. The irony is that that is exactly what
we found when together we arrived at a cold-water
apartment where he had thought to hide himself,
forgetting he had spent time with a certain young
woman who would sell her mother for ten dollars but

settled for five when it came to a man who had walked out on her even though she knew he had dollar bills hidden away, if not sufficiently well for her not to notice. To compensate for a shortage of limbs, my new-found detective friend carried a revolver but when we knocked on the door the man just looked surprised. Perhaps he thought we were Jehovah Witnesses come to tell him he wasn't one of the chosen. In the end he just shrugged and began to cry, which didn't stop my partner from kicking him where it hurt. 'Never trust a cryer,' he said to me later as we celebrated in a bar, one of several we visited, he having pocketed a bill or two from those we found.

It earned him a mention on page six of the *Telegraph* which is no big deal but was for him since it sent a stream of people to his door wanting him to follow people, find them, attack them, whatever they could afford, knowing he wasn't expensive and had got his name in the paper. For some reason he thought he owed me something. I count on people who think they owe me something. So it was that he dropped me a note, misspelled and with a stain which could have been from anything but smelled like vomit, spelling never being a

qualification for private investigators while drinking
was.

Being more presentable than a one-armed, one-
eyed Irishman, and, as I liked to convince myself, if
with little evidence at times, with a newspaper behind
me, I was ushered into a room so large that it seemed to
have its own weather system, hot by the open fire and
cold where I was sat. There was a chandelier and a
grand piano as if a set for an opera, not that I am given
to people singing rather than talking and in a foreign
language to boot.

We'd run the story for weeks but, like Ed
Quigley, it had lost its legs. People went missing all the
time, sometimes because they wanted to be missing and
sometimes because they would turn up in the East River
someone having put them there or having put
themselves there. Don't get me wrong. The Hudson did
just as well. Like the cops we received hundreds of
notes saying she'd been seen in the Bowery, on 5th
Avenue, downtown, uptown, only she was really black
or a prostitute or in the circus or a mistress to the mayor.
If she had been any of those, we would have had a story.

As it was it was dead, except it would maybe be a scoop if I could find what happened to her.

It was the mother who came to talk to me. She sat opposite, with a rustle of clothes and a cloud of perfume. She immediately began to cry. I had no idea what to do. Should I put my arm around her? No. That might be misunderstood to my disadvantage. Should I offer commiserations? No. That might imply her daughter was dead, which she probably was except I couldn't say that. One arm had a theory. He had been told she had been pregnant and gone to see someone who would help her deny it. That was it. No names. No place. I could hardly put this to her mother, or she would have sought her out and thrown her in the East River herself.

'You are a newspaper man,' she said, somewhat redundantly.

I confirmed her suspicion as she fiddled with some eyeglasses as if she wouldn't believe me until she had stared in my eyes, somewhat bloodshot, I confess, after an evening, well, the most part of a night, matching drinks with a woman who said she had information though she forgot it after the first few glasses.

'You know people.'

Living at the top of the Park evidently didn't sharpen the mind. I agreed with her. I did know people.

'People who wouldn't talk to the police.'

Right again, and often with good reason.

'They might know.'

'Might know?'

'What happened. Where she is.'

'It's difficult to know where to start.'

'You have no, what do they call it, leads?'

'Plenty of leads. The problem is that they go nowhere. Before she left…'

'Went missing,' she corrected me.

'Went missing. Did you have any sense that anything was wrong?'

'Wrong? Why would anything be wrong? She had everything.'

Everything except, perhaps, a reason to stay. 'So, no sense that anything was different.'

She looked off into space, though not, it turned out, thinking to answer me.

'She was engaged. To a banker.'

That was her proof that nothing was wrong, and I had to admit that going from rich to richer must have had its attraction.

'Your husband ...' I began.

'My husband?' she said, as if I had just farted in a church. 'What does he have to do with it?'

'He's her father,' I replied, equally capable of redundancy, except there was a flicker of something, lips suddenly tightening, eyes narrowing.

'He's in Boston.'

'Looking for her?'

'Work,' she snapped, as if I were simple.

'Right,' I replied, as if I should have known.

'How long has he been there?'

'How long?' It was a simple question but evidently not one she was interested in answering. 'Did he and your daughter get on well.'

'I beg your pardon.'

'No arguments, then.'

'I did not invite you here to pry into our family. My daughter is missing. Since you wrote those pieces, I assumed you might be someone with contacts, with some experience of …' For a moment her eyes appeared to fill with tears, but she was back in control in a moment.

'If you have nothing … If you know nothing.'

'Do you know how many people go missing every day in this city?'

'I am not interested in how many. It is my daughter who is missing. I think, perhaps, that will suffice.'

Suffice? What would? Then it became evident I was to leave. She stood up and a man glided across the floor toward us, a butler looking better dressed than I ever would. He could have been using Plimpton roller skates. I remembered how we ran a piece when the *Scientific American* called roller skating "propulsive divagations upon polished floors." The *Telegraph* specialised in mocking scientists, but this seemed a good description of the butler's propulsion.

She took a few steps and then turned around. 'You are useless,' she said, and left the room, the butler pointing me toward the entrance hall, itself larger than my apartment. Well, I had been told that before and there have been moments when I have believed it myself.

What happened? What happened was that her body was discovered a week later, in Boston. Draw what conclusions you wish, though I know what I think. As far as the New York cops were concerned Boston was another country and besides the bitch was dead.

So, a rich girl had died. That was what made it news. The same day she was found, a dozen other New

Yorkers were discovered in alleyways, apartments, abandoned buildings, staring at nothing, whatever dreams they may have had ending in a gutter, on a hotel bed crusted with blood, in a bar, amongst the trash of a country never quite catching up with the happiness they pursued. Nobody ever asked me to write about them.

As to the one-eyed, one-armed detective, it turned out he was not wrong about the abortion, though he never suspected who might have been its cause. But he had never seen the expression on a mother's face when I asked the simplest of questions. It is the simplest questions that sometimes open a door that other people would prefer remained closed.

Before she was found I set myself to discover where she might have gone, taking myself to Blackwell's Island in the East River where there is a lunatic asylum for sixteen hundred women, thinking maybe she had ended up there. Who would have thought there could be as many? I had been there before. It was a favourite haunt for reporters in search of a story and a possible place where anyone might disappear, or be made to do so. It is not a pleasant place, but pleasant places rarely make a good story. To begin with, it was cold and I saw several girls, their clothes wet through as though they had been pulled from some communal bath, standing in front of an open window, shivering. It turned out they had been, cleanliness being next to godliness, or at least a way of cutting down on fleas, nits, whatever, and because shit, piss and blood had got stuck to them as they were locked away to make them sane. There was a smell about the place which was part rotting food and part despair.

On my way in I had seen a line of women linked together with a rope passed through wide leather belts, shouting out obscenities. There was one in a straitjacket and another who turned in circles. This was a world unknown to those just across the water unless they read the occasional story brought back to amuse, for I had never read anything that gave a true sense of this place. On their clothes were the words Lunatic Asylum B.I. (for Blackwell Island). The sound I recall from that visit, beyond the mutterings of the truly insane, the sharp orders of those set to watch over them, and the occasional scream, was that of doors being locked and unlocked by those who carried key chains around their waists. Some of the women, I gathered, were injected with morphine and chloral.

There was a sign which read, 'While I Live, I Hope,' which was as neat a summary of the human condition as you could find. This was a charity institution in which I saw no evidence of charity, here, at the heart of a city with its new statue celebrating liberty, though that statue had supposedly originally to have been erected at the entrance to the Suez Canal – 'Egypt Carrying the Light to Egypt.' I was there when the *Isère* arrived with the statue on board, significantly in pieces. I was there again when Grover Cleveland presided over the dedication, the parade diverted past Pulitzer's *New York World* which had led the campaign to build it. There's a paper knows how to build its circulation. According to Cleveland it was a symbol of how Liberty would enlighten the world. It could have started by enlightening those who ran the Blackwell's Island lunatic asylum.

But I had a particular reason for being there, finding one lost woman among sixteen hundred, all surely lost in their different ways. I was told about one who had been brought in some days before, claiming to come from Cuba, though few seemed to believe her. Apparently, she spoke no Spanish. I was not allowed to talk to her but saw her across a room and though she wore the same drab as the rest of them, and her hair was tied in a single plait secured with a piece of red cloth, I recognised her, though it took a moment before I could believe my eyes. She was a reporter for the *New York World*. I knew better than to show I knew her because, unless she had suddenly lost her wits, I was sure she was here for a reason that had nothing to do with insanity.

I'm not a believer in women in newspapers. It is not that I think they should stay home and dust their homes, but it can be rough. I should know. Articles on fripperies are fine enough but not many would fancy going where the real stories are, wading through mud, literal and metaphoric. I made an exception, though, for Nellie Bly, though that was not her real name she choosing the American option of masquerading as what she was not. It turned out that she had convinced the police, a judge, and a doctor that she was out of her head. So, she was an actress as well as a reporter. She then allowed herself to be committed to a place that was unlikely to cure the insane but might be the cause of losing sanity. Even so, I had little understanding of how terrible it was until I read her articles. This was a place of such cruelty that it was hard to imagine it was tolerated. There is much vice in New York, dark crimes, and corruptions, but seldom masquerading as kindness. This was not a place where people were cured. It was what the French call an oubliette.

The *World* got her out after ten days. I doubt I could have taken two. She appeared before a grand jury and thus accomplished what none of my articles had in all the years I had been writing. She had something I didn't have, and I told her so when I met her. She shrugged. 'I saw you,' she said, 'thanks for keeping quiet.' I nodded. 'What next' I asked? 'I'm going round the world to beat Jules Verne's eighty days.' And by God, she did.

CHAPTER SIX: MY CITY

By now you are thinking New York one of the circles of Dante's hell. That's because I see things. I know there are thousands, millions maybe, who live normal lives, working regular hours, raising kids, who knows, even going to church on Sunday. There are those who get off a boat, start in a tenement sewing buttonholes and then work their way up to making coats or shirts so they have enough to move to the top of the Park where there are no peddlers, pickpockets, shoplifters, women looking for customers, being a long way from 25th Street and drinking rooms, though they could find them on the guilty third tier if they fancied a trip to the theatre. They get maids, just off the boat themselves, have men who will take them downtown to their factories, have a place in Far Rockaway, stage weddings for their kids which cost a hundred thousand dollars. They exist. Maybe they cheat their workers, save on fire precautions so that every now and then a score or so burn to death, but they've realised a New York promise. And if they have there are others who think maybe one day they will, too. So, they turn up to work each day, washing dishes, cleaning toilets, peeling potatoes, wheeling carts, lifting barrels convinced that starting at the bottom means they are already on their way. They should start a revolution. Instead, they tip their hats to those they hope one day to be. But hope was the last thing out of Pandora's box and there are those who hope themselves to death. 'While I Live I Hope,' indeed.

And if there is violence, what city can grow without friction, one race against another, one religion. Besides, this isn't one town. You come from another country, what do you do but settle down together and mark off what's yours from what's theirs. Italians, Germans, Chinese, Irish, each eating what they used to eat, singing songs they used to sing before they arrived in a land which they set out to make over, so it seems like the place they left. Jews, Orthodox, not Orthodox, distrusting each other; Catholics, spawning children and hating the Protestants who are busy despising those who think confession will lift guilt from men who were born with it; Masons with secret ceremonies threatening death to those who reveal what they get up to, which is greasing one another's backs and nodding to the

magistrate in a particular way to get off lightly. And
above it all a faint smell of horseshit and smoke from
brown coal.

But it's growing. By God it is growing with
buildings thrown up and torn down. Nothing is
permanent. Everything is changing. There are those in
Castle Garden whose very names are rewritten by
officials who can't pronounce what they are told,
waving on those with no right of appeal if they want the
right to stay. And what are those they left behind to
make of having to address their letters to what must
seem strangers? Transformation is what New York is
about. You change to survive and prosper. The problem
is that not all changes are for the good. Read William
James. Pragmatism. If it works, it's good. That's the
way of things in this city. Is it right? Well, that's a
whole other question.

Is home a word that can be used by those who
come here from somewhere else, as most New Yorkers
do, as they walk around their heads tilted back as they
look up at hotels and offices which seem to reach to the
sky? Does it await the birth of children fluent in the new
ways, the routine of a job, the slow drift into a new

language in a place in which neighbours are strangers and treat you as such?

No, the wonder is not that there is violence in the heat of summer, in a place where a man's word is not what it was once was. The wonder is that something else gradually happens as little by little people come to accept that the sun doesn't rise, as it once did, above a field sown with potatoes, but is fractured by concrete and steel, in this place of multitudes, with languages clashing, faiths clung to and betrayed, marrying out to breed those who will know nothing of the past and come to despise it for how lucky, they are told, to have been born to such promise as is embodied in a place whose very name, New, is a sign that they are its true inheritors.

So, am I a cynic after all? You might think it goes with the territory, and there is some truth in that. To begin with, I am not the only newspaper man who believes all politicians tend to reach into other people's pockets to keep themselves in power, that being their primary aim. As to businessmen, they have the same tendency to think that dollars are a measure of a man and that dollars belong, of right, in their own wallets rather than the pockets of those they like to call their customers. Look at these dresses. Would you not like them to be yours? In truth they are made by working girls who must provide their own sewing machines and who are dismissed when trade is poor and hired back only when it serves, but consider the stitching and the fine cotton, no longer picked by slaves in a part of the country we do not talk about except that numbers of its darker citizens have taken to fleeing a land of cavaliers and cotillions, to labour here, even as they are not welcome in the brightly lit stores where others are invited to consume, not noticing the while that they are themselves consumed. Buying and selling is what we are about. Everything has a price. Including us, all of us.

I concede that it is better to have than to have not, that ambition is not a crime and that there is a sound to my city, yes, my city, which is indeed the steady hum of hope for without it, Pandora aside, where is the lifeboat that will shelter us from the storm. Tomorrow will be better than today, and for many it is, for enough to make the slogans have a ring of truth. It is just that my dealings are too often with those for whom it will not, as with those who care nothing if others must pay the price of their own climb up the greasy pole.

There is a poetry to New York if also a prose, brutal and direct. Never forget, though, from whence these people came. They sailed an ocean to get away from places where they were the victims of history. Here, they can make it, and if they can't make it here then they can move on because they are told there is a continent to claim, somewhere else, an emptiness to fill, a destiny to follow, land to be settled once those who already live there have been moved on or eliminated, and who were here long before some Italian voyager set foot on land, some English adventurers or religious zealots, some Spanish conquistadors in search of gold, some Frenchmen in search of beaver, some Germans in flight from revolution, some Swedes looking for a territory as cold as their own, some Dutchmen who speak as if they had phlegm in their throats.

As for me, I am a reporter, an observer. I like to feel that I stand aside and watch a game played out, a plot yet to be revealed. I am not supposed to be involved, to step in to deflect a blow, allow feelings to dominate thought. Yet who is not involved? Zola said that a writer should be as cold as a vivisectionist at a lecture, but I have seen a body dissected and can assure you I was not cold at all. Can I really be when I see a city, a country, similarly dissected by those who revel in division, are ready to corrupt and damage to their own advantage. Is violence, perhaps, a natural product of the unsubtle energy of a nation still forming itself, rushing to complete what it convinces itself is its right and fate? A baby is brought forth in pain, it's mother's scream piercing the air. Can we expect any less of a city or a nation? As that mother will forget her pain so, perhaps, will we.

We are told we do God's work. It's right there in the Declaration, even as God is not supposed to meddle with government, the same Declaration that tells us that if things are not working out then we have the right to revolt if liberty proves no more than licence. There are times when I think there is a case for that with corruption in high places. Remember Grant, blind to the Whisky Ring, to Crédit Mobilier, the Union Pacific Railroad's scam which reached up to the Vice President, to Gould and Fisk trying to corner the gold market, to Belknap taking bribes from Indian reservation suppliers,

something, I guess, that would have registered with my
employer. Hasn't the Senate been called The
Millionaires' Club because that is what they are,
millionaires, though not from what they are paid to do.
The Constitution speaks of domestic tranquillity. In my
job I see little of that. I don't deal with Senators. Matters
of state are for others, except that crime on high casts its
shadow, sets the tone, provides a paradigm, grants
permission. What is the connection between charging a
bar owner for earning his living, a man relieved of his
possessions at noon on 42nd Street, taking "commission"
from city contracts, a knife in the ribs in the Tenderloin,
and light-fingered Congressmen, a Vice President
enrolled in graft? A matter of scale. At least the
criminals I deal with don't pretend they are anything
else, merely claiming to share some of their money with
a community itself happy to collude when government
shows so little interest.

Well, there you are. There's a statement of
where I stand, able, perhaps, to diagnose sickness but
with no skill to cure it, unless writing about it may itself
be a cure. Certainly, there are moments when I justify
myself along those lines. On the other hand, much of

my time is spent telling stories of no consequence, finding ways to entertain, make myself noticed so that I can move on up like everyone else. If New York were not what it is how would I have a job at all? Which is why I am no reformer, why, I confess, I revel in its unashamed nature. It is as though my fellow citizens are saying, 'This is how we are; why would you have us any other way?' And there are moments when I would say as much myself.

Yet there is another New York, of course. There are winters when people flock to Central Park, a sign having been lifted to signify the ice strong enough for skating. There are springs when flowers appear in the cracks and crevices of slums so that, for a while, they seem a kind of hanging garden as other people ride in cabs with no particular place to go beyond the pleasure of movement in a city in truth never still, the drivers in top hats secured against the breeze, while people on the El watch life pass by, albeit seen through steam and cinders.

Then there is Lillian Russel, born Helen Leonard, whose husband was arrested for bigamy. She is beautiful and has a voice that could turn you inside out. She performed at the Weber and Fields Music Hall on 29th Street and at the Abbey's Theatre on 38th. I saw her at both, though was dismayed when I saw her cycling in Central Park with Diamond Jim Brady, saloon owner turned crook, dealing in doubtful railroad stock. There was a reason he was called Diamond. He collected them, an enthusiasm second only to his love of food, his gargantuan meals at Rector's Restaurant being legendary, he having a particular liking for seafood, beef, indeed for practically anything. I dreamed of rescuing her, but she had offered no sign of wishing rescue not least, it was said, because her appetite was the equal of his.

I confess I had a liking for the world to be found at the Haymarket at 66 West 30th Street, known as the jewel of the Tenderloin, where you could eat, dance, drink and indulge in other ways. It looked like a theatre from the outside, and had been at one time, but inside was a regular carousel of noise, movement, light, along with activities of a kind that drew men and women for reasons other than dancing, though this was only a step from the Ladies Mile, with its fancy stores. The women, I should say, were often of a kind unlikely to be found in polite society, but no one went to the Haymarket for that. Men would buy champagne before slipping off to more discrete areas in the upper floors, curtained off from those who might inhibit the kind of activity they had in mind. Admittedly, there was theft, too, mostly by the young women who hardly counted it theft in the circumstances.

Those women who were not professionals were permitted free drinks, perhaps in the expectation that they might become such or at least leave their moral principles along with their checked coats. The owner paid a regular two hundred and fifty dollars a week to those in the police who might otherwise show too great an interest in what was going on.

Did I visit this place? Why of course I did. Did I climb the stairs with a young woman clutching a suspect bottle of expensive champagne, to disappear behind a curtain? I did not, champagne being more than I could afford and a glass of beer not being acceptable as an alternative. But I did dance, and I did drink, and I did sing, knowing that the next day I might be in a morgue looking down at the grey skin of some wretch who had despaired of this life or been eased from it at the whim of those with no music in their souls, indeed with no souls at all.

CHAPTER SEVEN: D.C.

'You want off the story?' he asked when I got back from my tousle with Tammany. 'Maybe we should back off a piece.' This was not one of the great crusading journalists, you understand.

'Maybe for a while,' I said, meaning permanently.

'How about you slip down to Washington?'

'Washington. What in heaven's name would I be doing there?'

He had the grace to look a little embarrassed, not much, mind you, but enough so that I knew it wasn't his idea, or not his alone.

'Take a look at the Bureau of Indian Affairs.'

'The what! Isn't it enough that I'm going to have to trek half the way across the continent without I get to bore myself to death beforehand?'

'Or you could run your head against Tammany if you'd rather. Maybe they wouldn't kill you, who knows. Maybe they'd just rearrange your face.'

'I'll check things out a bit more here,' I said. 'I've more than one source you know.'

So I did, but they could read the papers, too. So it was that I found myself in Washington, with its new Washington Monument sticking its finger into an angry sky having taken forty years to build, constructed, it was rumoured, in part by slave labour which seemed apt enough given that the man himself, like that other founding figure, Thomas, yeoman farmer, Jefferson, had owned slaves of his own, and done more than own them the rumour said.

Here, in the nation's capital, were to be found French Flats, on L Street, where Count Pierre de Chambrun, great-grandson of the Marquis de Lafayette, lived. The new electric streetcar runs up 4th Street NE to Michigan Avenue NE. $1.25 would buy a week's pass, but I wasn't staying a week. I was staying as short a time as I could get away with, though I was booked into the New Willard Hotel on 14th Street and Pennsylvania

Avenue with its marble columns which made it look
more like a mausoleum than a place to sleep and which
was out of my league, except word had come down that
I was already booked in so someone must have had an
angle. Ulysses S. Grant used to drink there but then he
drank everywhere. So it was that, within a day of
arriving, I found myself pushing open the door of the
Bureau of Indian Affairs in a city which had nothing
more going for it than that it was where power sat, and
sat pretty heavily, like its buildings.

The capital was better than I recalled from my
last visit. But that time I had been there in the middle of
summer and did nothing but sweat from sunup to
sundown and then all the way through the night. I knew
bribery and corruption were no less powerful here, but it
wasn't palpable. They spoke in quieter voices. Things
were more discrete. And here you didn't notice the poor.
There were no tenements that I could see, but then I
didn't go looking for them and there were places that
people went to feed their darker appetites and they
weren't hidden. There was Hooker's Division right on
the National Mall, named, so I was told by a hotel
employee with slicked back hair, after the Union's

General Hooker who had thought to position it where Congressmen could slip out between bribes. There was money here just as there was money back there, but here it favoured elegance no matter its source. Things moved more slowly and deliberately, electric streetcar or not.

As ever, I wasn't supposed to be able to read the reports sent back to the Bureau, not really. But, as ever, there were ways around that and the ways it turned out were much the same here as further north, despite the accent of the clerk I did business with where else than in a bar. He preferred that he should bring the papers to me rather than have me come to the office where people would ask him questions he would rather not answer. So, I spent a pleasant afternoon or so sitting in a park and watching the carriages glide by.

He would stroll toward me clutching a package that anyone but a blind man would know was contraband. He held it so tight that in New York the low lifes would have come from blocks like mice to cheese, except I had discovered that mice don't like cheese having a preference for peanut butter. He sat down beside me on a bench, of which there were none too many, since why should anyone be given a free seat to sit on, and slid them across to me. Why he thought this was any easier than making a formal presentation I don't know. There we were, out there, where anyone could see us.

As soon as he had handed them over, he stood up, looked around, in case anyone hadn't noticed anything strange as yet, and then strode off, returning an hour later to take them back inside the Bureau.

What I read was an extraordinary catalogue of betrayals, greed, exploitation, disregard on a scale I would never have suspected. I don't know how but somewhere, deep inside, part of me still believed in all the Presidents, except this one, all the Senators and Congressmen, except those I really knew about. I believed in the system, simply assuming that the likes of Croker had momentarily expropriated it for their own purposes. Well, it seemed there were plenty of other folks into the business of expropriation and, in this case, who knows, maybe it meant real trouble, but since that trouble was likely to be a continent away who gave a damn. That seemed the implication of it all.

Anyway, there were no notes here of the supposed messiah, at least not in the first reports I got to read, with carriages passing to and fro along the great boulevards designed for a future not yet arrived. But there was ample evidence that what Tammany effected in New York, Congress, or its constituent parts, effected in Washington while the agents of government seemed no better than precinct captains. What surprised was how many honest men were, nonetheless, warning against possible apocalypse, though for whom and by what means and when was by no means clear.

I read where a former Indian agent wrote of the land of the Sioux nation, with the confederated bands of Cheyenne and Arapahos, stretching from Yellowstone in the north to Arkansas in the south, from the Missouri River to the Rocky Mountains, and how that had been exchanged, under compulsion, for a reservation of sixteen thousand square miles. He wrote, too, of the disappearance of the buffalo and, like the man upstairs, I knew how that came about and how much it earned for who. This report seemed to suggest we might be in for something bad as the Sioux fought back, going to war again, for in that same document it laid out that they got half the beef we had promised them in whatever deal was made.

Meanwhile, politics was doing its little, too. The agent, who had worked at Pine Ridge Reservation, wherever that was going to turn out to be, was pushed out when the Democrats came in. Nothing strange about that but, according to him, out went all the Indians he had worked with and in came those he wouldn't trust one bit.

There was another report, from a general no less, that pointed out how the government had failed to fulfil a whole list of its treaty obligations, and talked of last year's crop failures. There had been a drought and nothing much seemed to have happened to address it. Acts of God lie outside legal documents. Then the money that was to have come from the Chicago, Milwaukee and St Paul railroad seemed never quite to have arrived, or never in the right amount. And there was more. No money for the ponies handed in, as agreed in '76. No cows, as there should have been by that same agreement. No seeds and tools, though they were in the treaty of '86; no rations, under the same, no annuity supplies as under the '88 treaty. And on and on and on. And this from a general.

I was there three days and not one of the documents I saw told any other story, but I still saw nothing of a messiah or a dance so maybe my contact had failed to get his hands on the relevant papers, or perhaps this was no more than rumour, no more than the fantasies of a man who kept himself to himself and dreamed of Mormons and Indian braves running Tammany. Except there had been pieces in the papers. I had paid no attention at the time but now recalled there had been a scare or two, though why anyone would have worried about a dance escaped me, the only ones I had seen being on stage with a crowd of women showing their legs, with brittle smiles on their faces, singing about love with a wink and a leer, love not being the kind celebrated in valentine cards which made a fortune for Esther Howland back up in New England.

But it made me think. Living in New York turned the world around so that you got to believe that things that were important there were important everywhere. There was nothing like going on a trip, no matter how short, to tell you otherwise. Who knows,

maybe the Big Chief was right. Maybe America was
what was out there and what we had in New York was
what people brought with them when they came across,
and not the best parts either. I still remember a man
staring at a dying Indian woman, shouting his name,
'Schwartz! Schwartz,' as if she would be impressed by
it, hear its poetry, when, in her mind, if there was
anything at all, was a poem which sounded something
like, Comanche, Arapaho, Kickapoo, Osage, Apache,
Delaware, Sioux, Algonquin. She had her own story, so
why should she be interested in ours or some book the
first part offering tales of slaughter and the second peace
on earth.

Until that trip I hadn't thought much about
Indians beyond they were in the way and killed people
on and off and took down the Fifth Cavalry when they
chose and were not in favour of mercy, or whites, come
to that. To tell the truth, the trip itself didn't change
much since all I saw was one mad Indian driving a
wagon and singing to himself and an old woman sitting
on the ground, staring round the edge of the world until
she took it into her head to close her eyes for ever. It
didn't change much, just showed me two who weren't

143

concerned to scalp or rape or shoot people and who
were not much more than what we had left once we had
swept on by in search of land or silver or gold or a
dream of tomorrow. I had realised that these were
people who didn't have a tomorrow. We had taken it
from them because it was so necessary for us to have it.
I didn't really think this then, but it occurred to me now,
reading these reports that fluttered in my hands as I sat
there in Washington where decisions were made, and
cash exchanged that decided everyone's future.

There was another document I read, the last as it
happened because someone had begun to ask him who it
was he met each day, having noticed him, as a blind
man would have done, skulking around like a spy. This
one was from a Captain at Fort Bennett in South Dakota
and talked of how Indian children were taken to be
educated in the east, made to grow crops unsuited to the
soil or climate and that the boundaries of their
reservation were not those they had agreed to. They
were to be tidied up, dressed like us, taught that
everything they knew was valueless and everything we
did was fine. There were some photographs of before
and after, from some Indian school in Pennsylvania, that

were supposed to show how much better they were when they had been Christianised but which to me made them look like they had lost their souls.

On and on it went. Did anyone expect something to happen because of such reports? Maybe things had happened. I still had no real idea why I was off on this venture, other than that a half-crazy man decided I should be. But I had begun to get interested. Maybe I was going mad myself, but I had begun to think that maybe he was right. Perhaps the Indians were the story, at least more of the story than men stealing whatever they could from people content to sell their votes to the highest bidder. Besides, what kid doesn't thrill to the dime novel, to stories of what lies where the sun sets? It was only April since guns had sounded along the Oklahoma border and everyone with a wagon, a horse, or a good pair of shoes had rushed in to claim land that had been set aside for the Indians. Some, it was said, got in before the guns fired, sooners. Well, there was a metaphor if you wanted one. So maybe it wasn't just New Yorkers. Maybe we all came here to grab what we could, possess our souls by possessing whatever was

145

on offer believing short cuts available for those with the wit to seize them.

He left me, scared to death and making me promise not to mention him, as if I had any intention of invoking some clerk as the source of any evidence, as if I had any intention of using it, at least as it stood. I made enquiries, though, while I was there, to see if there were any in Congress who cared a tad about any of this and found what I had expected, namely that the Indian was on nobody's agenda, except as some problem to be got rid of by whatever means came to hand. And I could be pretty sure that what was true of congressmen was true of the readers of the *Telegraph*, and if it had not been for an owner crazy for Indians I wouldn't have stayed another day. But I did stay another day, and another, too. And by the time I left I had a taste to go out to the Badlands and see what I could see.

Was I converted, then, turned around? I was not. This was another story and if it all came to nothing so had dozens of others. I got paid either way, and a good deal more than the compositors and machine operators working on the *Telegraph* at two or three dollars a day, working a sixty-hour week. Nobody was much concerned with how long I worked just so as I turned in usable copy. All the same, I could see how maybe there was something here even if I couldn't think why I was the natural person to write about it. Write about what? I wasn't even clear how I could turn this into something anyone would want to read over their Kellogg's Granola, a product, I learned, and wrote about once, inspired by a religious zealot called Sylvester Graham who thought that anything tasting of anything would inflame sexual desire, and if you've tried Granola you can see how it wouldn't do much for your sex life. The paper got more letters about that than anything I wrote about corruption but, then, nobody from Kellogg's was likely to track you down and break your legs if they took exception to what you said.

CHAPTER EIGHT: TWAIN

The railroad was fine, which is to say the smoker was fine, which is all anyone need bother about just so long as you arrive on time. Nor was I the only hack to be making my way to Connecticut, which otherwise was where I figured cows and sheep came from, if they didn't come from Brooklyn whose fields were closer and didn't need a rail fare to get to.

There was a dinner with all the big chiefs of Hartford, not just the insurance boys but the fellows from the Colt works, where they made the gun that had killed the Indians my boss seemed to love. In the afternoon I had been to the Church of the Good Shepherd, on the Southeast aide of Wyllis Street, which is not the kind of place I would normally choose to be seen but, there you are, a newspaper man has to chase the story wherever it goes. I liked the church, though. It was commissioned by the widow of Samuel Colt, the man who sold revolvers to the Texas Rangers in the Mexican American War, after we stole Texas, and it showed. He sold them to anyone who wanted them in

the civil war. Its porch was decorated with Colt
revolvers, carved out of stone, and the cross up above
was formed by rifles. I would have suspected someone
here had a ripe sense of humour, except that the idea
was his wife's who thought this the best way to
celebrate Sam, who had devised several different ways
of killing people. It was designed by the same man
responsible for Twain's house, Twain being a man
whose books I loved and who could smell the stink of
the nation as well as any newspaperman before had
done. And he was a newspaperman, which is what
made the trip more interesting and inspiring. After all,
if he ended up a millionaire there were others waiting in
line. And I was prepared to stand right at the front.

That evening we gathered at the city hall on
Market and Kingsley, built in the Greek Revival style
unaccountably loved by American democrats. They
were all dressed up in evening wear, except for us and
we were kept off at the side, except for the
photographers who as ever got to be right up front.

I kept close to a hack from the *Courier* who at
least knew the names of those who waddled past. Truth
is in the details, so they say. Get those right and invent

the rest. There was money in this burg, and it was plain
for all to see. That's America, for you. Make your pile
and then wave it under everyone else's nose. And, since
they were in insurance, they plainly made their load by
not paying out on fires, landslips, floods, accidents.
Here was half the world betting against catastrophes and
these were the merchants who cashed in when they
failed to come along and fought not to pay out when
they did. They had tables that told them when people
would die and of what. I didn't have a policy myself.
There was no one to benefit when death came along.

Twain was late, so I edged on in with the others.
They had roped off a piece at the back of the hall, so we
were close enough to smell the food but not actually eat
any of it. On the other hand, someone had been smart
enough to lay on a bar and, as a result, when the
speeches started not too many of us were in any
condition to make sense of what followed. Which was
just as well because I doubt that much sense was talked.

Then, suddenly, the waiters came around with
garlands of some kind made from vines, as near as I
could see, and each one of these worthies stuck one on
his head as if this were a meeting of the Greek gods. At

last, he gets to his feet, America's one true genius in my
book. He lived in this great house right next door to the
woman who started the Civil War, Harriet Beecher
Stowe, but my buddy from the *Courier* explained that
she had mostly gone off her head and was liable to jump
out of the bushes at you if you went too close, doing so
regularly with Twain who, as a result, was thoroughly
disenchanted with the heroine of the Civil War as well
he might be since his family once owned slaves and he
had been a confederate soldier, though only as long as it
took him to get out of that and everyone else's army.
Now, here he was, a director of an insurance company.
It didn't quite square with the man whose books I read.

'Gentlemen,' he says, and not talking to us you
may be sure, 'Hartford is a remarkable city. The Colt
Company manufactures guns, and we insure the people
that are shot with them. It's the perfect machine.'

They laughed, though whether that was what he
wanted or not I wasn't quite so sure.

'America, gentlemen, is like a train. It is full of
steam and is hurtling across a continent and we are all
ticket-carrying, fare-paying customers, but we haven't

the vaguest notion what the destination is. Some say we're heading for a town called perdition; others say it's New Jerusalem, by way of New Eden, New Paradise, but not we can be sure, New York.'

At this there was laughter, the one thing guaranteed to get a laugh anywhere but New York being New York.

'We are not the engineer on this train, nor even the conductor. We travel in hope and expectation, this being the two names imprinted on the front of our train. We travel hoping we shall not be derailed along the way, especially if our companies happen to have insured against such an eventuality.'

More laughter.

'But I don't see a sign of New Jerusalem or New Eden, as much as I stare forward against the smoke and steam. No, I see New Speculation and New Graft and a worship of the Almighty dollar.'

At this there was a strange sound, a kind of intake of breath, doubtless because this was a worship that united most of those around the table, wearing the laurels of the gods. They worshipped on Sunday but being men of deeper and more considerable faith, worshipped Monday, Tuesday and all the rest of the days of the week as well.

'Have you ever looked at a dollar?' he asked, not expecting a reply. 'If you do, you'll find an eye staring right back at you. And a pair of compasses and a pyramid. Nothing strange to many of you, I dare say, those familiar with the secrets of the east; those used to the building trade. But to most of our citizens, a mystery.'

There was a stirring in the hall, two hundred Masons clearing their throats.

'I'll tell you a story,' he said, changing tack, as no doubt he was used to doing when he sailed on the Mississippi if he chose sail over steam and the wind against him. You could hear the sigh of relief that he was going to give us a joke or two.

'I have seen strange things in this country. Before I was sixteen I'd seen abolitionists hanged and beaten to death; I had seen attempted rape.'

153

People looked around to check that there were no women present. 'I have seen people dig in the earth for silver and stab each other in the back if they didn't find it, or their neighbours did. I have seen vigilantes shoot and beat and stab and hang. Dammit, who's the man says this isn't the greatest country in the world!'

Damn me, if half a dozen people didn't cheer at this and a whole bunch of others look at each other to see if it were called for or if they were right in the first place when they got to thinking he should maybe be lynched himself.

'Fact is,' he said, drawing on a cigar he had been holding in his hand, 'I started with nothing. I was born in a log cabin. I guess I should have been President by now if things had worked out as they should. Lacked the bare faced audacity, I dare say. Even so, I guess I've done all right. And looking around it seems to me that much the same could be said of you.'

More cheers, this time.

'America,' he said, raising a crystal glass that shone in the light from a whole row of chandeliers.

154

'America,' they chorused back.

'Whatever was it went wrong?'

They were silent again. It was like watching a concert where the whole orchestra is controlled by one man who can make them play or be silent.

'Just joking,' he said, and there was another cheer. 'Looking around I can see there is nothing wrong here.' Another cheer. 'We all look pretty comfortable to me, wouldn't you say?' Another cheer. 'So long as people keep on paying their premiums.'

'So long as they keep on paying their premiums,' echoed a man at the top table, as if this were a popular song and he had just been reminded of its words.

'But what happens when the reckoning comes?' No cheer this time. 'And what of those out there without a nickel to their names? What of those who were slaves? What of the Indians whose land this once was?'

My God, it was catching, this stuff about the Indians.

'But didn't we take this land and make it bring forth corn? Did we not dig down and find coal and copper and silver?' Applause. 'And where would we be if we were like those who saw no purpose in tilling the soil or digging in the earth?' Applause. 'I have sailed down the Mississippi, the spine of America. It is tricky to navigate having sand bars and contrary currrents. There are villains on the boats that ply their trade, gamblers, women whose virtues do not include needlework. There are those running away and those running toward. It is an image of the country we sail upon, gentlemen. There are catastrophes to be sure. Boilers will blow up. My own brother died of such.'

A silence fell upon the room. Those in insurance prefer not to hear of disasters, while it seemed improper to be told of a family tragedy at a celebration.

'Nothing, though, was ever gained without a cost. Do we not know as much? But one of those injured in that same accident recovered and sails that river to this day. We thrive on adversity'

One man began to clap only to stop when others failed to join him.

'Especially in our profession,' he added. This time several clapped no doubt suspecting a parable about the virtue of those who dealt in risk, albeit financial rather than physical.

'There was a man,' he said, 'and this man only had one leg. And he met a tinker who offered to buy it from him. But if I sold my leg, he said, how would I move through the world and discover other places and other people? If you sold your leg and I gave you silver for it, why would you need to move around, replied the tinker, artfully. So, he sold his leg and to this day he sits at home, counting his money. America,' he shouted, lifting his glass. 'Nowhere like it in the whole world.'

He sat down amidst great applause. They had heard the story they had been waiting to hear. Was he not their very own clown and licensed jester? And yet there were one or two who looked a trifle puzzled, even those who patted him on the back and then turned away. But there was sufficient drink on hand to dull all questions and he was followed by a succession of other speakers who praised his speech and told jokes of their own, rather less obscure, and rather cruder, to be sure.

And what was I to make of it, who was supposed to write a report? I made of it that I was not alone in smelling what I smelled. As I say, Twain was a director of an insurance company, hard as that was to imagine, but he was also a man with an eye for hypocrisies. Did characters not carry guns into church in *Huckleberry Finn*, a church surely very like the Church of the Good Shepherd? How did he keep his moral balance?

Well, to hell with that. Back to the hotel, where the gas lamps hushed away, bourbon looked the colour of mahogany, crystal glasses rang out a peal of bells and there was the warm stench of humanity giving up on itself. I was not alone, for there were others of my breed but this wasn't the night for getting drunk with them. This was a night for getting drunk on my own, which is cheaper, on the whole, and better for the soul. It's bad enough to be on the slide but a deal worse for every Jack and John to see it happening.

The next morning, I had an appointment with Twain at Farmington Avenue, though I lost my way a couple of times, bourbon not being conducive to a sense of direction. His house was huge, set back from the road and made of, what, cedar wood? It was brown at any rate and had more rooms than I could guess at. It had pointed gables and tall chimneys and was shaped a little like a boat stranded on dry land. I remembered what I had been told about Harriet Beecher Stowe, but she didn't jump out on me. I don't know why he had agreed to see me, except he was a man who knew the virtue of publicity and had been a newspaperman himself after all.

I presented myself at the front door and was led to the top floor, a billiards room, and waited there for the great man to arrive. And, yes, I did think of him as a great man, certainly as the only really great writer we had. I had never been able to read the New Englanders who went on about sin and God and nature and sent me right off to sleep whenever I gave them a go. Twain was different. He had been places, done real jobs, in a way I thought American writers should. And he managed to laugh at things and take them seriously at the same moment. Also, I have a thing about people who come from anywhere out in the great yonder, beyond not only New York state but the several states that come after it. It's as though I suspect they have a secret I would like to learn, except I had never discovered it when I lived in one and he came from the next state to me when I had wanted nothing more than to get away.

He came in at last, bending forward a little, with his tussle of white hair lit by a golden glow from the early sun slanting down through a window.

'Sit down,' he said, though in truth I hadn't yet got up. 'Coffee,' he shouted over his shoulder. 'God knows if we'll get any, though,' he said, sitting down himself. 'It's just something I say when we have guests, but it's not worth gambling on whether it will come or not.'

'I enjoyed your speech last night,' I said, not really knowing what to say but needing to get things started.

He looked up at me, sudden and sharp, like a bird hearing something nearby.

'Enjoyed?'

'The ambiguities.'

He paused, and then seemed to relax a little, 'ah, the ambiguities. Pierre or the Ambiguities.'

I must have looked puzzled because, in an irritated voice, he said 'Melville, Melville.'

'Ah,' I replied, not knowing what he was talking about.

'Worse book he ever wrote.' Then, changing direction, and shifting himself in his seat as though to indicate he was doing so, he added, 'what you want from me, then? A story? A joke? A reminiscence?'

Why I said it, I don't know. It was the way to get myself shown the door. But I said, 'this seems a pretty grand house for the man who wrote *Huckleberry Finn*.'

There was a pause, and I could see his eyes narrow. There was a clink from the door and the maid backed into the room with a tray.

'I'm not sure we'll be needing that,' he said, even as she placed it on a low table between us before leaving, pulling the door closed behind her.

I wondered whether to withdraw the remark but could no more think how to do so than I could think why I had said it in the first place.

Then, at last, he said, 'seems to me you've got your own version of me and hardly need me to mess it around for you.'

'No,' I started to say, but he paid no attention.

'I'm to be sentenced to poverty, is that it? Write for nothing. You write for nothing?' It was not a question. 'There are things I need to do. Things that cost money. I had the first telephone, you know.'

I did.

'You interested in moving pictures?'

'You said something last night, in your speech,' I began.

He paused. 'You read *The Gilded Age*?'

Yes, I had certainly read *The Gilded Age*. It was my Bible. 'It's still like that? I asked, knowing, of course, that it was.

'Son, human nature being what it is people will always cheat and steal and lust after other men's wives and there is nothing you nor I can do about it. But when it comes to cheating and stealing and lying, well, this

country has honed and perfected the art. It is our
destiny to lead the world in this. We have the best
judges money can buy, and don't let anyone tell you
otherwise. There are people who if they did an honest
deed by mistake, in a sort of inadvertent way, would fall
on their knees and ask forgiveness from the Worshipful
Temple of the Captains of Industry. If this was a ship
there would be those prepared to bore holes in the sides
for ten cents a time, fifteen below the water line, and
they think this was why God put them on earth. They
pile up the loot and then squat on top of it convinced
they can bribe their way into heaven, as if they believed
heaven were their natural destination. You ask about
my money.'

'No, I …'

He waved a hand. 'No, I can see how you might
want to ask about that in view of what I have said. It
isn't money that corrupts the soul. It's not even the love
of money that corrupts the soul. It's the power it brings.
I have no power and want none. There are things I want
to do. There's a typesetting machine has got me
interested, to the point it will doubtless bankrupt me.

There's things I do with money I won't go into. There are times, though, when I think you may be right.'

About what? I hadn't had the vaguest idea what I was saying. I certainly hadn't come there to accuse him of anything. This was Mark Twain. Simply being there would have been enough for me. Asking him for the time of day.

'I don't yearn for the past. There's no purpose in that. If you'd been as poor as me, you would know there's no virtue in poverty. And don't get to believing that everything's fine just so long as you keep clear of the city. I saw enough cruelty and greed and violence before I was ten to last me a lifetime. All the same, there are things you know when you're young that you forget when you grow up and that if we remembered maybe we would be a mite different. Coffee?'

I had forgotten the coffee. He lent forward and poured, his ebony walking stick leaning on the chair.

'Do you take sugar?'

Somehow I felt everything was a test. 'No,' I said.

'Something in it?' he asked, with a wry smile, and produced a silver flask, unscrewing the top and pouring what turned out to be whisky before I had time to say yes or no, before I knew which was the right answer.

He leaned back in his chair and swallowed the coffee, his own now enriched like mine.

'Now let's see. You're from New York. The *Telegraph.*'

I nodded.

'Well, it could be worse. I haven't read it that much, but there are worse.'

'Yes,' I began.

'I've never stopped being a newspaperman,' he said, staring up at the ceiling. 'Reporting is what I do. People think I make it up but all I have to do is keep my eyes open, describe what I see and then stretch it a little.'

'I'm not sure ... '

'Oh, you're going to tell me you don't stretch it at all. Just say everything that happened. Well, maybe you're right. Maybe that's when reporting stops and fiction begins. It's all in the stretching.'

'You're ...' I didn't know quite how to put it, or even quite what I was trying to say, 'you're pretty much part of the community here.'

'Pretty much,' he said before I had finished.

'An insurance director and so on.'

'And so on,' he repeated, with a smile.

'Yet, you don't really share much with them, do you? You were just saying about businessmen.'

'Oh, they're not so bad, I dare say. They're not selling snake oil, you know. They're not selling Florida real estate. They're doubtless as honest as a man can be while trying to weasel out of paying what you promise, and that's not for publication. You live in New York. I live here. But if you're asking do I hobnob with them on a daily basis, no I do not. I turn up every now and then to keep them honest, watch them swallow a juicy worm so they will maybe one day wake up and find a bent pin in their throats. No, there are far worse than them. Far worse.'

'It's 1890. We're only ten years from the turn of the century. What do you think is in store?'

'Why, more of the same unless you know different. There'll be machines, of course, and those with ten million dollars will have a hundred million and we will rule the earth because we already own more of it than almost anybody else. And now we've got through killing the Indians we'll find someone else to have a go at, just as we freed the slaves and then invented other ways to make them slaves again. And we'll elect bigger and better rogues who'll spend half of their time telling us we are the greatest people in the world and the other half doing things that prove the opposite. And reading books and going to the theatre will be against the law because what have such things ever done but stir people up to be discontent. And there'll be preachers and congressmen and inventors who'll promise to bring heaven on earth if we'll just let them have a dollar or two apiece. And we will believe them because, edged into a corner, we believe anything. Most folks came to this country because they were gullible enough to believe that things would be different instead of which they have turned out to be much the same, just a long way away from where they had been before.'

'You are serious?' I asked, to be truthful not so sure whether he was or not.

'Me? Serious? Why would I be serious? No, look around. As you so delicately implied, I have done all right for myself and if I can come up from a log cabin to this, well, there can't be too much wrong with the system, would you say. Dreams, nightmares, what does it matter what the currency. Trading is what counts. Is this the greatest country in the world? Absolutely. Is this the most corrupt country, cruelly deceiving those who believe in it? No, not really. It's just that, big as it is, its promises are bigger, and people will always blame themselves for not realising them because if this is the greatest country in the world then it must be them that's at fault. You pay a price for that. So, you tell yourself that all is for the best in the best of all possible worlds when you know it isn't. You believe every charlatan that comes your way with a magic ingredient, telling you it is new and improved, thereby confessing it was rubbish before. This is the land of the confidence man and confidence men only thrive when there are people without confidence in themselves but with a need to believe. We made people believe. That was our sin. And there is no way of curing people of that.' Then, as though coming out of a reverie, he said, 'you're not going to use any of this, are you?'

'No,' I said.

'Doesn't match the picture, does it. Don't worry, I'll give you a story or two you can use.'

And he did. He told me how *Huckleberry Finn* had been planned as the Christmas book in 1884 but someone doctored one of the pictures so that an avuncular figure appeared to have an erection. So, this most American of books first appeared in England. I couldn't use that, of course, but he told other stories. They were pretty funny, too. It wasn't the funny stories I remembered, though. It wasn't that he was a bitter old man, indeed he seemed to me to have a childish belief in the future, outlining half a dozen crackpot schemes that the simplest person in New York would have seen through in an instant. It was as though he had two ideas in his mind that ought to have cancelled each other out but didn't. It was as though he could pick the confidence man out in a crowd and then allow himself to be fooled just the same.

He offered me a cigar. I don't smoke but accepted it. It seemed rude to do otherwise. He could see I was lost, though, and clipped it for me, a smile on his face.

'So, how do you like Missouri, then?'

I came from Kansas, so you're not supposed to like Missouri. 'Remember Lawrence,' you are told when Quantrill's raiders came to town slaughtering because they didn't like those who favoured slaves. 'I'm from Kansas,' I said.

'Ah. Old, mad John Brown. Home of Buffalo Bill's family.'

Buffalo Bill again. There would have been the beginnings of a fight here if I had given a damn. 'In God we trusted; in Kansas we were busted,' it was said. Well, I didn't choose to stick around and had no interest in fighting yesterday's battles.

'I left,' I said.

'I can see how you might. People get us wrong, though. Especially people from the east. You're not one of those, though, are you.'

'You think we're different, then?'

'Hardly. There's just more space here. And space gets a man to thinking, though somehow there's a bias against that. We make guns here. Well, I guess you know that. The problem is that guns cut short the thinking process which is what took those boys into Lawrence and set John Brown on his way to the madness of Harper's Ferry. Well, it's been good talking to you. I guess if I ever read what you write about me, I won't recognise myself, but few people do see themselves as others do. So, good luck to you. And I wouldn't take up smoking. I can see it doesn't agree with you. And watch out for my neighbour. She might take a liking to you.'

I took the train back to New York, having, if only for a couple of days, cleared my mind of the daily clutter that passed for life there. When we parted, he gave me a pen he had got from some inventor who claimed it would last for ten years. It carried its own ink supply. It ran out after I had used it for no more than half an hour. I don't know whether he gave it to me to underline what he had said about promises and disillusionment or whether he really believed it would see me into the next decade. In the event it didn't even see me into the next state.

CHAPTER NINE: THE ACTRESS

I moved into a new apartment that had nothing to recommend it but its location. It was a streetcar ride from the office, not fashionable enough to be expensive but just fashionable enough not to have to wade through discarded cabbages and drunks lying in the street. I even had hot water, occasionally, when the boiler decided to operate and the janitor wasn't off somewhere betting on the horses or selling keys to our apartments which, semi-fashionable or not, tended to be broken into with such regularity that I took to leaving abusive notes for the thieves which achieved nothing more than persuading them to piss all over my chairs.

Mostly I lived alone, though occasionally I overcame my scruples and allowed some woman to come in and wrinkle her nose up at what she found, and what she found was only partly me. I can deal with loneliness much of the time, figuring I disgust myself less often than I am likely to do someone else. I even prefer it, and not just because it allows me to live in the kind of squalor that would dismay me in someone else.

There's just me and whatever's on my mind. Me and
my habits. Me and my despairs. Me and my disgust at
the world.

But every now and then it's not enough and for a
time I convince myself the world could be different and
that one way to make it so is to find a girl. So, I find
one, not always looking in the best of places I have to
admit. And she moves in and for a while it seems to
work. There is someone waiting for me other than a
barman, or some informer ratting for a buck.
Everything's fine, until it isn't, and it isn't, eventually,
because I can't figure out what I am doing or why I am
doing it. Then there's a scene, or I stay out for rather
more drinks than are strictly necessary to ease my way
through the piece I am writing, and then there's an
earthquake and when I wake up, she has gone and I'm
alone again and liking it. It's a mystery. For a few
years you can take it without asking questions. Then,
one day, when you're vomiting at three in the morning,
or waking to see the grey light battling through windows
frosted with dust, you ask yourself where this particular
train is taking you and why you are on it at all. And
even a visit to the bridge won't do the job, won't clear

the lungs or the brains or the soul. It doesn't happen that often, just enough to bring me up short.

There was one girl, an actress at the Strand, and not bad at that, though she never played a part of any size. The odd thing was I later saw her in a play called Tammany, or, the Indian Chief, by someone called Mrs Ann Julia Hatton. It dated to the last century and felt like it. It had music, if you could call it that. If I'd paid any attention, though, I would have been a bit wiser about the origins of Tammany Hall. She still smelled of the greasepaint when she came home at night. Sometimes I would meet her at the stage door, along with the other no hopers looking for a bit of glamour. She was young enough to convince herself she would still make it someday, and perhaps she would. She had talent enough, as it seemed to me, though what talent did it take to be in the melodramas. Not a lot you had to admit.

This was not a great time for theatre, unless you liked to hiss the villain or were one of those who thrilled to see a train cross the stage, smoke and sparks flying out. One time I went and the man sitting next to me threw up. No one paid any attention. People in the gallery had fun throwing peanuts on those below, and New York was proud of itself as the symbol of American civilisation. Sitting in a theatre and watching a man dressed in black throw a pregnant girl out in the snow, while men in the audience spat in the aisle and women screamed, didn't say much for civilisation, any more than did running the risk of a blackjack on the neck walking home afterwards for those that couldn't get a carriage. But she was different, or so I thought. Beautiful, yes, especially up there on the stage, but with a bit of go in her if not the brains I might have wished.

Young as she was, she had been married before, to an actor. The problem as far as he was concerned was that he had only a fraction of her talent and there were those who let him know as much whenever he stepped on stage. There were times when I thought she might have had a child, but, if she did, she never told me such. I don't know what gave me the feeling, but I had it just the same.

There were Sundays when we would go in the park, and she would fantasise about some future she could see, and I couldn't. With the sun shining you could almost believe it might come true, but it lasted no longer than it took for her to find someone a notch or two above me, which didn't take much effort. Then she saw a different future. I can't say I blamed her overmuch, or even that I was too dismayed. I wasn't looking for a settled future, even one with an actress who would never be settled because of what she did. All the same I was sad when she left, sad but not destroyed.

For a time, I came across bits and pieces that reminded me of her: a ribbon, part of a broken comb. If I was really cured I suppose I would have heaved them in the trash. I didn't, though. I kept them in a box, in case she came back, knowing all the time she wouldn't, knowing even that I didn't want her to, that it had been a mistake much like all those other mistakes that didn't seem like mistakes at the time but turned out that way simply because time passed and things went bad as things do when time passes. Perhaps it is a natural law. Perhaps not. Maybe I just chose the wrong people, that's all.

You could say that I am not good at relationships with women, and I would have to agree. They look for something different, permanence, maybe, commitment, while I have no idea what I look for. Certainly not the above. It doesn't go with my job. Maybe it is because I remember my own parents who were held together by nothing but circumstance until even that proved insufficient. I guess I like living on the edge, and who would settle for me being out at all hours in places that didn't fit with ideas of the domestic, with furnishings and millinery, clocks on the mantelshelf, cosy suppers around an open fire, visits by relatives. Or maybe I secretly yearned for just that but could never admit it because it was a trade I could never bring myself to make.

CHAPTER TEN: ICE PICK, KNIFE, GUN

Don't ask me how I got the book, but I got it.
Well, I got it for fifty dollars and for knowing who to
ask. And I didn't get it in New York, this being a
careful man, but across the line in Jersey. But I got it
just the same. There it all was, written out in a careful
hand. Names, amounts, shares, the whole thing. It's
funny how someone so careful in some things – the
writing was done with pride, each letter deliberately
formed, each entry precisely aligned – could be so
careless in others, careless not so much in putting these
details down in the first place, or keeping them where
someone could stumble on them and sneak them away,
but careless of his own sense of himself, morality,
whatever you want to call it. Because what was this that
I held and went through for the best part of one night
and then another, but a catalogue of vice and villainy.
Here was someone presumed, though not by me, to be
serving the public when in fact he was part of a
conspiracy that reached out in every direction – down to
a sad girl in a six-by-four room in the Lower East Side,
up to a mansion on 54th Street, from the cop on the beat

to the mayor who watched it all as if he were proud of what he was doing to the city he was supposed to lead.

The question was what to do with it, in the sense that a book with so many names was garbage until I could prove it was more than a piece of fancy writing, a dime's worth of fiction. The names were there right enough but what were names? I needed people to go on the record and going on the record was like requesting a swift transfer out of life. Who was it said he could move the earth if he had a lever long enough? Well, I could do with a lever and the book wasn't it, at least the book on its own was not.

The first thing I did was copy the whole thing out, and more than once. Simply having it in my possession was like wearing a target. Indeed, it crossed my mind that maybe that was why I had been given it at all. To set me up. Except why would they bother when a couple of boys off the boat could do the necessary without being given a reason. Nonetheless I felt better when one had become three and two of those were where I figured even they wouldn't get to find them.

I had a piece of luck. Sometimes the machinery that seems to run so smoothly, as if money were oil enough to keep things going, gets a little grit in it along the way. And a little grit came along in the form of Daniel Murphy. Getting a cut was fine enough provided the cut you got reflected the importance you granted yourself, as well as that granted by those who gave it to you. But every now and then there was someone who rated himself rather higher than others might and figured the way to handle that was to see there were fewer snouts in the trough. I guess they learned it down on the farm some place. But when one gets nudged out of place the whole lot of them stagger a little and reorganise themselves to get back where they figure the best of the swill is. And that's a useful moment to be around because suddenly there is not just one person feeling he is getting less than he should but a whole line of them feeling bitter and looking for someone else to give the push,

Daniel Murphy thought he deserved more. The system has two ways of dealing with that. Either it looks such a person up and down, stares into the future to see whether this one is going anywhere or not, and gives up a little more of the loot in case one day he remembers who helped and who did not, or they decide he is better off dead and set about to make the necessary arrangements. In his case they decided the latter, but he got wind of it and took out the two men who presented themselves through his bedroom window with an ice pick, it is said, though it didn't strike me it would have been their weapon of choice.

That raised the stakes. It was like poker. There was a pause while the other players did their calculations over again. There were those who recognised inevitability when they saw it – in this case in the form of two over-sized bruisers trying to squeeze through an under-sized window who obliged by dying -- and there were those who decided they would rather not. They looked at their cards again, still as strong, as it seemed to them, but with a whisper of doubt now that had not been there before. They tried one more time, throwing some more money on the table, in the form of a young man said to be an expert with a knife, of which he had so many about his person that he would have been wise to avoid any magnets carelessly left around. But artistry is one thing and a revolver another and

Daniel Murphy proved once again a law which should have been known even by a young man proud of his art, namely that a bullet will travel faster than a knife. Your bid, he might have said, as he rolled the said young man into the East River and went for pie and potatoes at his favourite restaurant, followed, at a discrete distance, by two men he had hired at rather more than their worth, to ensure that no one else should come creeping up on him, or if they did would be greeted by his representatives.

At this point the players decided that their cards were perhaps not as strong as they had first supposed and accordingly threw them down, permitting him to sweep in the stakes that had been so carelessly tossed on the table. But things were not to be so easily accomplished. Common sense should have told them that the easiest way to accommodate this new player was simply to raise the rate of tax they exacted on the rest of humanity – and no one, in New York, could think himself free of taxation since bribes must be recouped and hence every bar, every store, every business of any size paid its dues to men who obliged by collecting weekly from their establishments. But rather than do this, with its attendant problems of negotiation, of recording, persuading, they chose to divide the same amount along slightly different lines. And the result of that was new resentments, for nobody likes a pay cut and these were all men who reckoned they knew their worth to the cent. As a consequence, more men tried to squeeze through more bedroom windows, more young men, who fancied their special skills only to find them not quite special enough when push came to shove, confronted other men on streets which began to run with blood.

At such moments danger signifies its presence as dogs are said to anticipate earthquakes in California. And danger is not good for business in so far as it brings rather greater attention to bear than is good for those who prefer that their business be conducted in the shadows with what passes for decorum among those whose idea of such is to be polite when killing people.

Even the friendly newspapers find themselves hard put not to deplore a rather too regular bloodletting on the streets of a city which announces itself as a harbinger of the future. Accordingly, meetings were held, decisions made, victims selected, and those who had thought themselves secure suddenly found themselves superfluous to the organisation they imagined themselves to have sustained with loyalty, or if not loyalty with perseverance. Names were offered up, policemen released to practice the trade for which they had supposedly been trained, if you could call it training for new recruits to be taken around the bars and introduced to those who would supplement their wages on a regular basis and see that they were kept in food and drink on a cold New York day when, heaven knows, they were bound to be feeling a little hungry or thirsty what with turning the other way so often.

Not that such cases could come to trial, of course. Loyalty is one thing but there might be those who felt that in being offered as sacrifices such contracts as they had implicitly signed were perhaps no longer entirely valid. So, more often than not, they would frequently disappear, and not always to an afterlife, unless peeling potatoes in a Jersey restaurant or pioneering in Ohio could be said to be such, and there were those who said it was since it plainly had little to do with living itself. But there were some who resisted going west, in either sense, and thought, ungrateful beings that they doubtless were, to revenge themselves on those who so casually offered them up. And that was my chance.

I met more than a few of them and slowly laced together a whole cloth from the threads that spun out of their fear and resentment. They told me stories which fitted into other stories they knew nothing of, never being allowed to understand what it was they served and never caring, either, just so long as the dollars came their way. It was a world of winners and losers, and they knew which they were to be. There was a system in which even the victimisers were victimised, and I wasn't sorry when, after I had run two weeks' worth of articles, a message came sighing down the vacuum tube with my name on it and a single word scrawled in green ink: INDIANS! I recognised the imperative without an exclamation point. And suddenly I wasn't sorry to be going because I had come to feel that the whole enterprise had been sold and in some crazy way me along with it.

CHAPTER ELEVEN: TRANSFORMATION

I had begun to think it had been forgotten, though I had kept my eyes open for any reports, you can be sure, and there was the odd piece came in from the west. To my surprise there was a report of a messiah out in Nevada and even talk of a dance he had started that had spread to other tribes. But since this messiah not only went by the name of Wovoka, that made him sound as if he were straight over from some Polish village, but was also known as Jack Wilson, Jackson Wilson and John Johnson, he could just as easily have been an outlaw.

Anyhow, I found myself back in the office with a finger or two of whisky and, as ever, the fingers literal enough, being told that there was no way of getting out of this one.

'Who knows,' he said, 'maybe there's something in it, after all. And if there isn't, you'll dig something up.'

'Dig something up?'

'Well, why not? It'll make a change from what we've got right now. Tell us about the Bad Lands.'

'Bad Lands.'

'What do I know. That's your business, seems to me. Besides, Johnson'll bring back some pictures.'

'Johnson,' I said, guessing we weren't talking about a messiah. I swallowed and held the glass out, drinks in my experience always coming in multiples. 'Who in hell is Johnson?'

'Photographer.'

'What photographer?'

'You get to travel with a photographer. And not one of ours, either. Word came down,' he said, indicating the vacuum tube beside him and shrugging so that I knew he had nothing to do with it. 'Seems he volunteered when someone told him about the story. Besides, you saw Fly's pictures of Geronimo in *Harper's Weekly*. Went out to the Sierra Madre.'

Of course I had seen them. It was only four years back, but the *Telegraph* preferred words. Cheaper, I guess. 'And who is this Johnson?'

'His father was at the gunfight in the O.K. Corral out in Tombstone I'm told. It was outside his studio. He disarmed Billy Clanton.'

'He was already dying as I heard.' Everyone knew the story. 'Liked a drink,' though why I said that as if it disqualified him, I don't know. 'So why Johnson and not Fly?'

'Off somewhere in Mexico. Besides which, Johnson was recommended.'

I thought he said he had volunteered, but it made no difference. 'How long are we going for?'

'Long as it takes.'

'To do what?'

'I could say to find the story but since you and I know there ain't any, I should say just long enough to satisfy him and just long enough to file copy so that we can say it hasn't been a complete wipeout. And who knows, maybe it's a chance for you to dry out.'

It was a joke. We both knew that. He wouldn't have trusted any reporter who had dried out, being permanently pickled himself. He called out and the door opened. Here, it seemed, was the person I was to work with.

There was something odd about the photographer, not that I could figure it out then, though, if you had asked me to. He looked a little slight, as if a stiff breeze might blow him away, but I had come across his type before. I was sure it was only a matter of time before he started talking about his 'art' and 'texture' and 'angles' and all the gobbledegook they used when they just lined things up and pushed a lever or whatever they did. His hair was close-cropped, like a soldier boy's or a convict's, but there was a softness that wouldn't have served him well if he had tried for the Cavalry. His skin was sallow. We shook hands and his grip was about what I expected it to be. I had more than a suspicion I knew what his problem was but who was I to care, except of course that I would be sharing a carriage with him and maybe much else besides before we got back to where the air was thick enough to breathe again.

'Philip Johnson,' he said, in a voice not deep enough to reassure. I guessed he was no more than twenty, maybe twenty-five. The feebleness made it difficult to guess. If he had been at Tombstone he would have been twelve or so at the time so I didn't believe a word of that. Someone had sold someone a bill of goods.

'You've seen his stuff?' said Fickey, knowing I hadn't. Anyway, I wasn't much interested in what he had done before. I would as soon have done this job on my own but if I was to be saddled with anyone I would have preferred someone partial to a drink or two, someone I could talk to and go to sleep at night not feeling uneasy about.

'You made arrangements?' he said, meaning working things out about when I would telegraph, which of course I hadn't only just being told the jaunt was on. Anyway, the photographs were another matter, and I had no intention of getting involved in those.

'Sure,' I said, and looked across at Johnson. He showed no signs of knowing what we were talking about, which was all right by me. What did I care in the end? What did I care about this whole trip come to that?

'You been west before,' I asked.

He stared back at me as if I had no business enquiring.

'Can you ride?'

'Sure,' he said, though he didn't look that confident. On the other hand, remembering my own experience I wasn't about to push myself forward as some frontiersman, either. Riding was the last thing I intended to do. I had only had a pony when I was young for a week before it died. I rode it once and even then fell off. When it died, I felt relieved. Then there was my visit to watch a woman fall dead before she could be told she would rise again. That had about cured me of horses, the west, Indians, and pointless assignments.

'How much gear you got?'

'Enough,' he replied, in an irritated way. 'I guess you can leave all that to me.'

'Too true,' I said.

'Telegraphed ahead?' Fickey asked, not needing to, and knowing as much but not able to stop himself from asking as if he were a mother hen, which at times he was.

'Everything's in place,' I lied.

'Draw the money?''

'Sure.' As how could I when he had just sprung it on me.

'And sign for it.' This last was a joke that depended on knowing what had happened when I didn't and the two of us didn't talk for a month until the whole thing got sorted out.

There was a rush and thump from the vacuum tube and a cylinder dropped into the wire basket by his hand. We both knew where this had come from so that not opening it was a gesture of solidarity. We were all in this together, except that he would get to stay in his chair, with his whisky close to hand, while I had to set off with some callow youth where even now people got shot from time to time or killed by things had no right to be on God's earth.

As though he were reading my mind he said, 'you could get shot you know.'

'No other reason for going,' I said, and spun around.

'The tickets are with the money,' he shouted after me. So much for asking me if I had arranged things. 'And you'd best stick together.'

'Why,' I said, and then regretted it. 'OK.' The two of us were going to have to travel together so that we might as well be talking at least when we started out.

We walked through the office, and I offered to buy him a drink, but he turned me down. Had things to do. So did I, and I couldn't say I was sorry not to be taking a drink with someone I had got married to by the editor or the man upstairs. I tried to convince myself that this would be a change from trailing mobsters and breathing cigar smoke with a pen in one hand and a drink in the other, except that was my world and where we were going could be another planet, and not one I wanted to visit.

Perhaps we all live in denial, first cousin to betrayal. The best thing to do is to seize the day, but those are the kind of catchy pieties you find on the back page of papers which have mottos on the front page declaring, 'Truth and Justice with *The Globe*.' Ours says, 'Think Again.' God knows what that was supposed to mean. I doubt that thinking came particularly high for those who paid their five cents to read that some woman, in some country they had never heard of, had given birth to eight children, or that the new transit system was delayed by another year and those running it were under investigation. 'Think Again!' And that's the paper I write for. It was clear, though, that the old man upstairs was not about to think again so that I would have to go off on some fool's errand, not sure who the greater fool was, the one who read the Book of Mormon and believed what he read there, or me doing what he wanted me to do.

I met up with the photographer at the railroad station in Jersey City. He had two porters in tow, and a clutter of equipment. I wondered how he would get on when we got somewhere that didn't have porters, but there you are. We each had our job. I guess he wouldn't settle for the new Kodak. Too simple. Press a button and you freeze time. He was waiting for me, hopping from foot to foot like some flyweight boxer trying to avoid a looping right. I gave him a wave and I swear he almost came up and gave me a kiss he was so relieved I had arrived. I had had some things to do, not least keeping out of the way of certain people who had decided that I was the cause of their troubles and so arrived only a minute or two before scheduled. We piled everything in, the porters and me, since all he did was hop around and tell people not to drop things in a voice so high that it made me uncomfortable all over again to think that people would see the two of us together and get ideas maybe.

But we got everything in and then we were off with a jolt that sent both of us falling into our seats. It was four in the afternoon so that, as we pulled out of the city, we were chasing the sun. And that was what we were going to be doing for several days as we made our way across an America I had never really seen before, except when I was young and travelling the other way. So, we were travelling ever further away from New York and its smell, ever closer to something I had been told maybe had the answer to the conundrum of a country I thought I knew. At least that was what our proprietor believed, though in truth I suspect he was not entirely of this world hiding himself away as he did and communicating through a vacuum tube.

I had a book to read. Mark Twain, of course. My companion, for want of a better word, slept as we made our way across a land where the states were so many lines marked on a map as if geography meant nothing at all to those that drew them. Back in Europe borders were marked in blood. They were lines of exhaustion where people finally wearied of fighting but might begin again at any time. Here they were just a convenience and meant little enough to those who crossed them, except when slavery had been at stake. The lines pioneers followed were lines of desire. They went chasing some dream or other, looking for something they would maybe never find. But they chose the paths themselves. Sometimes they led somewhere, sometimes not.

The railroad shot out as straight as the Mason Dixon line. For those that went by wagons, and there were those still that did, there were ruts left by others, or a path marked out by the memories of Europe thrown out as they went having to lighten the load as the going got tough. But eventually they stepped off the map, as maybe I was about to do because, at least in my mind, Indians existed in some kind of space beyond the whites. And even if we had pretty well broken them, like some wild colt brought to heel, and even corralled them into reservations, or chased them to where no one else would or could live, they were something else, somewhere else, with something in their eyes we would never understand if we tried a hundred years. For some, they were vermin, on a level with rats. For others they were what we were before we got snared in a chase for something we couldn't name but thought we would get to hold in our hands. Certainly, money didn't seem to matter to them if it's true we bought Manhattan for a row of beans. If they were that simple, though, why had we been killing them rather than trading junk for their land?

I don't know when I would have found out about him if the engine hadn't blown a valve so that we stopped for a day and a night in a town that didn't even have a name as far as I could tell. Admittedly there was a hotel, with five rooms in it, and a bar, and I wouldn't be a newspaper man if I didn't make sure that we got one to share while others were left walking up and down and cursing or lying on the benches in what passed for the depot.

There was, then, a bar, though who it served unless trains blew their valves on a regular basis, it was hard to see. There were just two men sitting across a table staring past each other as if they had run out of things to stay. They made no sign of noting that two strangers had come in.

He didn't want a drink, he said. He would wash up, in so far as you could with no more than a jug of water and a bowl, and get an early night. Since it was only nine, I saw no advantage in that. There were too many good drinking hours to go. So, I went down and had a shot or two. Then I found I'd left my wallet in the room and, since they wanted cash with every drink, as if I would split without paying, I went up to get it. Which is how come I had as big a shock as I have had in many a year.

I walked in the room, not knocking since it was my room and why would I want to do that. He stood there looking at me, stripped to the waist and with the jug in his hand. Except it wasn't a him but a her and you didn't have to have very good eyesight to realise it. She just stood there looking at me while I looked at her, unable at first to comprehend what I was looking at.

199

For a second or so I guess I thought I had been saddled with some transvestite picture taker. But then I came to, at much the same moment she dropped the jug and snatched up her shirt. The jug hit the floor as I might have done if I hadn't stepped back and pulled the door closed behind me as though I had walked into the wrong room, as somewhere in my mind perhaps I thought I had.

I cannot begin to explain the thoughts that went through my mind. It was like I had landed in a different world, one like our own but not in ways you could work out at first. I had met him as a man, decided my attitude to him as a man, and now here he was a woman. Or perhaps he was something in between. I stood out there on the landing, with the smell of generations of dust in my nose and that of something cooking that I hoped was for the hogs I had seen in the street, and broke out into a sweat. They existed, after all. I had seen them. But seeing them was different from being with one. And yet, even in the instant I had been in there, that frozen moment when my eyes sent messages to a brain that seemed to have gone out to lunch, I knew that wasn't so.

As a man he had been feeble, laughable; as a woman, well, I was going to have to sort that out.

I couldn't begin to do that right away, though. For now, I went down to the bar again to have another shot. The barman, if that's what he was given that he looked like a cowboy who had lost his horse, set up a tab, no doubt seeing I was determined. The rail tracks ran straight down the street and as far as I could see there wasn't much more to it than that. Even so there was a hotel and a bar so that something must go on even if I couldn't figure out what it could be. But for the moment I had other things to think on.

I was in there I guess no more than half an hour when in she came. Everything had changed. In place of the pants and shirts she was wearing a dress, and if I had seen her strolling down Fifth Avenue she wouldn't have seemed out of place. She walked up to me at the bar, if you could call it that when it was no more than two barrels connected by a plank.

'Mine's a bourbon,' she said, putting her head on one side, and suddenly all the thoughts I had had when I thought she was some effeminate man went straight out of my head and a whole lot of other thoughts came in. But I guess she could see this happen because she sat herself down and when I joined her said right away, 'this doesn't make any difference.'

'The hell it doesn't.'

'I'm a photographer.'

'Until half an hour ago you were a man so how do I know you are any more honest at the one than the other?'

'I'm a photographer, all right.'

'Then why did you dress yourself up like Oscar Wilde to get a job?' though I knew, even as I said it, what the answer was.

'Because I wouldn't have got a job if I didn't. Name any other women taking pictures out here, or anywhere else come to that.'

'Even so.'

'Even nothing. You do what you have to. My father was a picture taker and I know more than he did but there's no one would give me a job, and if they did none that would send me where we are going.'

'Where you're not going,' I said, knowing even then that there was no way I could stop her.

'Please yourself,' she said, 'I'm going where I'm going.'

Then she sank the shot, as fast as anyone, and got up to go.

'What am I ...?'

'What are you what?'

'What am I to call you?'

She paused and looked at me as if trying to decide if it was worth talking to me at all.

'You can call me Miss Bridie.'

'Miss Bridie? Whatever happened to Jackson? You want I should call you Miss Bridie?'

'It's my name.'

'Maybe it is,' I said, not really convinced of anything about her except that the longer I saw her wearing a dress the less I could recall her wearing anything else because now I saw her as a woman, and not some failed man, I could see that she was maybe even attractive in a way, though her jaw was set firm enough for the male not entirely to have left her.

'You got a first name?'

'Yes, I've got a first name, but I keep that for my friends, and I can see you've set yourself against being one of those, so Miss Bridie will do.' Then she paused, and I could see she was rehearsing a speech in her head. 'Look,' she said, after a moment or so, flicking her hair behind her and staring me in the face, 'we've got a long way to go and I can see that what I did, well, it might have seemed, it was, well it was what I had to do but not what I chose to do.'

I nodded, meaning to be helpful, I guess, but she narrowed her eyes as though I had contradicted her.

'What was I supposed to do? Stay at home, marry some banker's clerk, forget what I wanted to do? You do what you have to.'

'You couldn't have told me?'

'And if I had?'

She had a point. What would I have done?

'If I had you'd have been no different than the
rest. You'd have settled for a man with half the talent.
You'd have told me that this was no kind of trip for a
woman.'

'But were you dressing up as a man before
anybody thought of this trek out to nowhere.'

'Sure, I was. Because it's not supposed to be
ladylike or some such. Mister, there are women out
where we are going raising kids where there's no water,
and husbands going crazy because they can't plough
dust. We don't blow away in the wind. We're here to
stay. I did what I had to do, and there it is. I'm off to
bed.' And so saying she banged her glass down, got up
and swung around so that her dress flared out. It gave
me a strange feeling. I looked around. The two men had
woken up and were looking at me as if they had a
question they wanted to ask. I had plenty of my own.

And what was I supposed to do? She was off to
our room but suddenly I presumed it wasn't my room

anymore, though why I thought that I don't know since neither of us had said anything. Nonetheless I got up and followed her, three or four paces behind, like her servant instead of someone who still couldn't get his mind around what had happened, even though all that had happened was that a man had become a woman.

She opened the door when I knocked, though why I had knocked I couldn't quite figure since I was the one who had got the room and paid for it.

'Yes,' she said.

'I'm coming in.'

'Oh, no, you aren't.'

'It's my room.'

'Seems to me you're on the outside.'

'What are we going to do about all this.'

'All what?'

'About you being a …' for some reason the word wouldn't come.

'Woman?' she said, helpfully. 'We aren't going to do anything. You've got a job, I've got a job and I guess we're both going to do them, wouldn't you say.'

'But you can't go around like that.'

'Like what?'

I was going to say that she couldn't go around wearing a dress, but what did I expect her to wear. I guess I was still thinking of her as a man who had somehow dressed himself up in a woman's clothing, and this despite the evidence of my own eyes. The image was still there somewhere, frozen, as I had seen her, the jug falling, my eyes falling, too, from the face to somewhere lower. And her hair had changed. Before it had been short. Now it was long, obviously a wig, except it didn't seem obvious at all.

This all seems easy to write down as though meaning to go one way I had decided on another but someone changing in front of your eyes is something I wasn't used to. Sure, people lied to me, all the time. As a result, I had learned to distrust appearances, but this was something different. An honest man turns out to be a crook. Fair enough. A crook turns out to be honest about some things, if not the main ones, and I had seen that. I had also seen for myself how a woman on a stage was not like the woman in your apartment, hanging her clothes on a line over the bath, but this was altogether more disturbing.

'Good night,' she said as I stood there, and closed the door. And from the other side she added, 'let me know if it's mended. I wouldn't want to miss it, after all.'

I went down for another drink, discovering that one wasn't sufficient in the circumstances. The two men had been joined by a third. Perhaps word had got around that there was a woman in town assuming that they hadn't figured that she had been a man half an hour earlier. Somehow they looked different now and I noticed they were carrying guns. We have guns in New York, plenty of them, but I had read a dime novel or two, including, once I had drawn the short straw of chasing Indians, Beadle's *Malaeska: The Indian Wife of the White Hunter*, published before I was born. It was by a woman and told me nothing except women should steer clear of writing dime novels. One thing I did notice is that in the dime novels those who carry guns tend to use them and here was I with nothing more I could beat them to the draw with than 150 words a minute of Pittman's shorthand painfully and expensively learned. Did you know it was this year they published the Bible in shorthand? The point of that being what exactly? For fast readers? Anyway, when I looked again they seemed to have lapsed into a sullen silence. An attractive young woman apparently left them cold. Did I say attractive? Well, yes, perhaps she was. She was attractive unless seeing her with next to nothing on had influenced me. And how had she concealed the fact that she was, what should I call it, full bodied. I guess she had bound herself around with a piece of cloth. You can see how my mind had begun to go on an excursion. Already I was reconsidering my attitude to a journey which had seemed no more than a pointless chore.

After a bit I went back upstairs and knocked on the door. She opened it. I could see where she had put a blanket on the floor. And that was where I spent the night so thrown by everything that I couldn't bring myself to object. It was a hell of a way to begin a journey.

CHAPTER TWELVE: THE RATTLER AND THE DERRINGER

As we travelled so the land changed. Back in New York there was no horizon, no sense of the land stretching away into the distance. Here there seemed nothing but horizon, curving round in a grey-mauve line. Later I learned that this was how Indians thought of their land. This blurred line easing down at either end defined the limits of their world. This was the space where they lived and somehow, as you travelled mile after mile, it seemed that there must be room for them as well as us. There was more nothing than something. There were more places that would be somewhere someday than were somewhere already. After a time, you couldn't look out of the window because nowhere seemed very different from anywhere else. It was just land. Thousands had set out west but there was no sign where they might have gone. They seemed to have been swallowed up in the vastness. Back in New York you were hemmed in. People crashed into you. Shouted. You got jostled. If you crossed the street there was a chance you would be trampled by horses. Here, there was nothing and had been nothing since creation's early dawn.

Every now and then, though, we would pass a gaggle of houses, like a bunch of birds that had settled down for a bit before taking off again. But it wasn't often that you saw such, except where the train stopped every now and then, mostly to take in water, I guess, though what do I know about trains except they use coal because a fair deal of it found its way into my eyes when I looked out, cinders still glowing as they rushed past.

Nobody seemed to get on or off and I couldn't begin to imagine what it would be like to settle out here, or why anyone would choose to do so, except out of some desperation. There were supposed to be towns and farms, land for all. Well, there was land all right but not a lot else besides. And no towns, at least no towns as I would have recognised as such. It just went on and on and I couldn't help but feel what loneliness there was out there, flying past me. Go west, young man, Horace Greeley is supposed to have said in the *Tribune*, another newspaperman who never stirred beyond Manhattan, except once to the Colorado gold fields. For some reason he was against drink, which didn't match with his profession. He lost in the Presidential election. Perhaps that's why, being up against a national champion when it came to a bottle.

They were an odd bunch on the train. We had a compartment to ourselves so that we only saw the others at meals. There were a couple of families who seemed as struck dumb by what they were seeing as I was, and then a bunch of men who I guess worked for the government judging by their clothes and drinking habits. No newspapermen, though, which was good news if there was going to be anything to report, which I doubted. And no newspaperwomen, either, which was even better news, though maybe the government men were women dressed up seeing that as the only way to rise to be Secretary of State or something.

She had transformed herself and was a pretend man again, though once I had seen the butterfly, I couldn't believe the chrysalis. I guess she recognised that the further west we went the more she would maybe attract the wrong kind of attention, though heaven knows there were predators enough in New York. She hardly spoke. I suppose she realised I was still trying to make sense of what didn't make sense. We both had books, though after a while I couldn't concentrate. Even Twain couldn't stir me. To my surprise she was reading a dime novel. Perhaps that passed for research with her. It didn't raise my opinion of her, though, even if I had read the same book or ones like it, but there are things men read that women don't, things men do that women don't, or shouldn't.

Then the sky turned yellow, and snow started, first a few flakes pulled away behind us but soon a flurry until there was nothing to see but whiteness lit by orange sparks. She had been silent at first, as if daring me to speak, but after a while opened up. I guess there was no one else to talk to and we were brought together by more than a train. So, the two of us declared a truce of sorts and after a while I began to learn a little more about the man I had despised and the woman I was almost beginning to like. There was nothing I could do, after all, and she showed me some of the stuff she had brought along. It was all right, I guess, though pictures always look dead to me. You could do more with words. The right sentence is better than the right photograph. It has a heartbeat. In a photograph people can't speak for themselves. There they are forever mute, and you must imagine what might have been in their minds beyond the discomfort of posing for someone who cares nothing about them. There was something irredeemably fake about those pictures, except she had some of New York and it didn't take much to imagine those crowds springing to life, the people rushing around as New Yorkers did, always giving the impression they have somewhere they have to be, someone to see. Nobody ever strolled in Manhattan. They were energy in human form and even the photographs couldn't entirely freeze them.

Turned out she was twenty-five and not twenty-one, her father's daughter in that he had been a photographer up in Connecticut, and not Tombstone, only he had died suddenly falling through the ice he was cutting for icemen to deliver in Boston. The grave is a cold place. So, the assistant became the principal. I wanted to know how come she was single, but she closed up when I asked putting her hand to her face as though to shield herself. Well, we all have our secrets. It turned out she had sold a picture or two to the *Telegram* and someone must have seen them. Then again, she was cheap and that always appealed to my employer who knew the value of a dollar.

'You ever been west,' I asked.

'Depends on what you mean by west.'

'West of Philadelphia.'

'Then, no. You?'

'I come from here.'

'So, this isn't strange to you?'

'You mean all this nothing going past the window? No, it's not.'

'You always wanted to be a newspaperman?'

'Once I decided not to go to sea on a whaler or slaughter pigs where I was raised.'

'So, no regrets.'

'About the pigs? No.'

'And whaling?'

'You've read *Moby Dick*.'

'Moby what?'

'No, I guess you haven't. Nor have most people. Anyway, it was a warning.'

Just then a series of jerks sent us sprawling. There was a squeal of brakes.

'You OK?'

'I'm fine. What is it? You think we're being held up?'

It turned out to be a cow that had had enough of chewing prairie grass and decided to throw itself in front of the engine. They didn't call the bit at the front a cow catcher for nothing. Anyway, it took a while before we could start off again and I stepped down. So did a woman further down the carriage. I barely registered her when she screamed. I was not the first to her but was in time to see the rattler wriggle away, sounding a warning but too late. My companion was close behind.

'A knife,' she called.

'Don't cut her,' I called.

'For her clothes.'

It seemed she had raised her dress in stepping down and the snake had struck high on her thigh.

'Something to tie,' she called. 'A rope, a belt, something.'

'How long before the next station?' I asked the conductor.

'Five hours.'

Five too many, it turned out. A piece of cotton was found, and her thigh bound, but it began to swell. Within two hours she complained of dizziness, failing sight, extreme pain. The man with her was plainly overwhelmed. He wrung his hands, barely able to watch. She vomited, her pulse raced, and her temperature rose until it was over.

I had been taught about rattler bites back in Kansas. They would hide out in prairie dog burrows, but in the summer you could find them almost everywhere. I remembered my father going on snake hunts. They liked the heat so why one was around as winter arrived who knew. Perhaps the train had disturbed it, the heat of the engine. Remedies, as I recalled, were whisky,

217

cutting, sucking the poison, though whisky, in prodigious quantities, probably killed more than the poison. The conductor told us she had died. We had retired to our carriage.

'How did you know what to do?' I asked. 'You come from New England.'

'My sister was bitten by a timber rattlesnake.'

'Did she survive?'

'She did. They are not so fierce as this one. But I set myself to learn what to do having failed to do anything but run for help even as she screamed.'

We fell to silence. Somehow human violence was one thing while the random cruelty of nature had always left me bewildered. Even in New York we have pit vipers and copperheads. There is a reason they are associated with the Devil. If creatures had been created to serve man how come so many of them seemed dedicated to biting, stinging, eating any man or woman they came across? Seemed to me that God had enough to account for when it came to poison ivy and ticks, without brown spiders, scorpions, alligators, sharks and mountain lions.

Having someone die like that, for doing nothing more than step off a train, was, what is the word, distressing, disturbing, shocking? There was nothing to be said, and we said nothing. It was a warning, though. I was back where things could kill you, and it didn't need marauding Indians.

As I say, it had occurred to me that she might have had another reason for dressing as a man, but I kept that to myself. I had known a few like that in the parlour houses in Midtown west of Broadway, or the French houses in the Tenderloin. There were papers published lists so sporting men would know where to go. You could buy them on newsstands. I had seen such women/men in the theatre, touting for trade in the upper gallery. The more we talked, though, as you will gather, the less I had been inclined to believe this, though I thought her masquerade unnecessary. More likely she would win us a free pass in that even gun fighters might give a little when it came to shooting a woman. You can see that my dime novel reading had begun to get to me.

As to the Indians, I had done my homework thumbing through back issues of the *Telegraph*. It turned out that the man at the top of the building had picked up on them and their dancing two decades before, though given that was in the far west and nobody in New York could care about anything a continent away I was surprised there was anything to be found. Apparently, it started with someone called Wodziwob, which made him sound as if he came from Krakow. What is there with these names? Which reminds me of a joke I heard. A Polish man goes to an eye doctor who asks if he can read the jumble of consonants at the bottom of a chart. 'Read it,' the man replies, 'I know the man.' That's a Jewish joke. I sometimes think all jokes are Jewish. Anyway, this Wodziwob went up a mountain and had a vision that the earth would move, and everyone would be swallowed up by an earthquake except that the Indians would come back from the dead, which is a good trick if you can carry it off. Tough luck on the whites who would stay gone. Mind you, if Indians didn't believe this crap apparently they would stay gone as well.

The dead would return on a train from the east, and I could sympathise with that since I was feeling pretty dead myself after days of travelling. His mistake was to put a date on the train. It would come along in four years from when he said this, which, to nobody's surprise but him, and those he sold the snake oil to, it failed to do, which was a special disappointment to a disciple who for some reason too deep for me to fathom also called himself Frank Spencer or Dr. Frank. That was it, a piece at the beginning, by someone who left the paper before I joined and was still revered as a man who could write three hundred words, mostly coherent, after a quart of whisky, and a follow up when the train failed to arrive giving people in Queens a laugh before going to work on the car barns for the Brooklyn City Railroad.

This time around word had come they were up to it again. That's where Wovoka came in, though he was less down on the whites. But all this was out in Nevada and there was no way we were going that far, which is how, as a staging post, we chose Chicago named for a kind of garlic, which tells you a good deal, though it's not garlic you smell there but cow shit and pig shit. Anyhow, that's where the rail line went. Time enough when we got there to figure where next. Besides, there'd be a few stories there we could pick up on in case the Indian one disappeared in an earthquake.

Things took a turn when we stopped for a while. She changed back into a woman for some reason known to her but not me. The snow had let up and a thaw set in so that water was dripping down silver icicles from the station roof. She had unloaded her equipment and I helped drag it under cover before we stepped inside to take a coffee, or what passed as such. There was a stove and we had two hours before we could move on, so I would have been happy to sit there. There was even a local newspaper, so local that the rest of the world might not exist. I say newspaper but it was no more than a single sheet with words crushed together, so it took an effort to read. What described itself as a town was called End of Hope, which sounded familiar and seemed about right if not likely to attract any settlers thinking of, well, settling. Small as it was it had this paper whose banner read: 'Everything You Need to Know about End of Hope.' It was about wagon wheels breaking, a man arrested for sitting in the street when drunk, a fire in a lean-to quickly put out, people being born, marrying,

222

and dying, though in truth few in any category. Even so, I settled in to read when her scream stopped me. I hadn't noticed her leave. She had gone out to check on her stuff only to find someone had stolen it. There'd been nothing about master criminals in the local paper.

It turned out that since the snow had only just started to melt it wasn't difficult to follow the footsteps. You didn't have to be an Indian guide to see how there were two of them, and none too steady on their feet. So, it was no surprise we found them in a bar. How they knew there were pickings at the railroad station wasn't clear unless this is what they did everyday with people moving on with no time to look for what they stole.

They were sitting at a table with the camera and stuff in front of them and a tripod propped against a chair. I hadn't quite figured how we were going to get it back other than asking for it.

'My camera. My tripod,' she said, maybe thinking that a statement of fact would set things right.

They pushed their chairs back with a squeal. When they got up it was clear they were a foot taller than her and had several inches on me.

'You'd best be on your way,' said the taller of the two, black hair combed back, his eyes narrowing to a slit. To underline his point he spat, and not into a spittoon.

'My camera. My tripod,' she repeated as though facts trumped spittle.

'Little lady,' he began, before the shot rang out. And it wasn't them. She was holding a Remington derringer, the kind favoured by women if women favoured carrying a gun as most did not especially, I would have thought, attractive women photographers from the East, if that is a category. Bullets from a derringer are so slow you can see them in flight, but not slow enough that you can move out of the way. And they can kill right enough. I have seen more than one sporting man in the morgue having angered a young woman by doing what she objected to, or cheated someone at cards, or simply looked at someone in a way they didn't like. She had fired in the air, or at least I assumed she had since both men were still standing, standing very still, suddenly aware that they were dealing with the unexpected in the form of a woman who might or might not think theft a capital offence. I knew there were two barrels on the Remington and so, I guess, did they because though she could only have hit one of them, they couldn't be sure which of them it would be. That being so, they made no objection when we gathered up what they had taken and returned to the station. I didn't talk on the way back but once we were by the stove, I found myself saying, 'You have a gun?' She looked at me oddly since of course I knew she had.

'Would you have shot them,' I asked.

'What do you think?'

'I have no idea.'

'Neither did they. That's the point, don't you think.'

'But I didn't know you had one.'

'That's the point, too.'

'Have you always carried one.'

'My dad gave it to me.'

'Before he went through the ice,' I said, immediately realising I shouldn't have said it.

Her eyes narrowed. 'Don't you have one?' she asked.

A good question since I had thought about it enough but always figured I would never be able to shoot my way out if I tangled with those I had to meet on dark nights. And if I did, I knew there would be those who would come after me to explain it was not my job to shoot. That was for those who had maybe trained in some school for criminals.

'No, though after seeing you maybe I should. How good are you? A derringer is one thing, but you couldn't hit anything much more than a yard or two away. Or are you an Annie Oakley? I saw her once in the Buffalo Bill Wild West Show.'

'Lillian Smith was better. And she was only fifteen.'

Suddenly I was dealing with someone I didn't know at all. She was along to take pictures. Now it turned out that not only was she a woman masquerading as a man, but she was a sharpshooter, or at least admired those who were.

'It seems to me,' she said, 'that if we are going out to take pictures of Indians you might do well to carry more than a notebook and pen.'

'Well, one thing I can tell you. That derringer isn't going to stop any Indian unless you're in kissing distance.'

'What makes you think that's my only gun.'

Dear God, I was dealing with a gun fighter. Then I remembered that Annie Oakley was a friend of Sitting Bull, and it was he that we were supposed to seek out, though that meant South Dakota which was a hell of a way from Chicago. Still, I was on salary.

We all knew that Sitting Bull was also originally called, Buffalo Bull Sits Down,' which is weird, if a laugh to those who didn't reckon anything to Indians except what they read in the papers. Indians have a thing with names. I checked them out, the Lakotas. There was one called Clever Racoon and another Red Shirt. Did he never change? More worrying was Kills in Woods. Mind you, there was a Fourth Ward Street mugger, part of the Charlton Street Gang at the end of the 60s, called Sadie the Goat. She used to work up and down the

Hudson. Then there were Hop Along Pete and Skinner Meehan in the Tub of Blood Bunch, so I guess the Indians weren't so odd.

The real puzzle for me was how could Sitting Bull get fistfuls of cash – I heard $50 a week -- for riding around the arena pretending to be himself when he had had a hand in the Little Big Horn before high-tailing it for Canada and then surrendering. That's why people in the bleachers shouted out and spat when he rode by. He even charged for pictures and autographs. Then it was back to the Standing Rock Agency where some divorced white woman from Switzerland, along with her lover's child, had decided to go live alongside him and work as his secretary and, who knows, maybe something more. That was when the Ghost Dance was going on and the question I was sent to ask was whether he was one of the dancers.

'I suppose you learned about guns in Tombstone.'

'Tombstone?'

'The gunfight.'

'The gunfight? What has that got to do with me?'

'Your father.' Then I realised that of course it had all been nonsense. Hadn't she told me otherwise? I knew it, but part of me wanted to believe. How could I still be naïve? I thought no one could take me in anymore. Well, it seems they could.

'Forget it. Some story I heard.'

She looked at me as if I were a child who believed in fairies.

'What would you have done?' she asked.

'Back there.'

'Would you have just given up?'

It was not an unreasonable question. Who knows what they are capable of until the moment comes? 'I'd have interviewed them.'

'Well, that would have terrified them.'

'There's more than one way of getting people to do what you want.'

'Yes, well that will doubtless do us a lot of good if we ever come up against some raiding party.'

Something shifted in the stove. A man appeared with a shovel of coal and opened the door. He poured it in and shut it again. 'Cold,' he said. It was not an invitation to talk. 'How long?' I asked. He shrugged and went out. The coal shifted in the stove.

'My name's John,' I said, feeling we needed to start again. She looked at me and I thought she wouldn't reply.

'Jane,' she said, 'though I've got another.'

'What is that?'

'Jane will do.'

So I guess she considered that maybe we were friends after all, though I wasn't so sure.

CHAPTER THIRTEEN: CHICAGO

I'd never been to Chicago before and never
wanted to. New York was enough for me. Even so, I
could feel something in the air. It was where our line
ended, and a host of others began. They seemed to have
had a railroad fever. Meanwhile, at the depot, there was
another fever, people rushing everywhere as if the world
were about to end, and they had to clear their bank
accounts first. I grabbed a porter to carry everything. He
didn't look pleased when he saw what she had dragged
across half the country, but there's a reason they are
called porters.

'You and your wife here long?' he asked.

I wasn't about to explain. He got us a cab,
though, and we headed for the Palmer House on Monroe
and State, which is the only hotel I had heard of. I think
Twain said he had stayed there. It turned out so had
Ulysses S. Grant, Sara Bernhardt, and Oscar Wilde,
though not together, I guess. It was advertised as
fireproof which was just as well because the original
had been burned down in the great fire, thirteen days
after it opened, a disaster which must have cost those in
the insurance business back in Hartford a dollar or two,

unless they had weaseled out of it. It was a good thing
word had come down that I was to have a generous
allowance because I quickly found how expensive it
was. If I tell you the barber shop had a floor partly made
up of silver dollars and there were gold chandeliers in
the lobby, you'll know what I mean. It was seven stories
high and had what it called perpendicular railroads
connecting the floors. Well, we've got elevators in New
York. There were also telephones, but since I didn't
know anyone in Chicago except a contact I was to meet,
that was just a swank.

When I went to check in the clerk looked down
at me when I asked how much, and I figured we would
have to turn around and leave or maybe share. I looked
at her and could see she knew what was going through
my mind. She shrugged. We stayed. I got a look from
the clerk but I'm immune to looks. Anyway, you can
persuade them with a little loose change.

I tipped two bits, partly because the porter, a
young man with a pimply face and inquisitive eyes, had
to drag along all her boxes and stuff, and partly to mind
his business. The room was big enough for a baseball
team provided they didn't mind sharing a bed because it

turned out there was only the one. She looked at it and said, 'there's a couch,' which there was, but I wasn't paying a ransom to sleep on it.

'It's big enough for two,' I said, 'and don't worry.'

'I won't,' she replied, 'remember, I've got a derringer.'

'We'll move out tomorrow. It's just the one night.'

'So, the couch won't be too bad. And I'm hungry.'

'We're not eating here. That would be a month's salary,' even though I could finesse the expenses.

So, we ventured out into a city which seemed full of saloons. I was later told that a fair number of city councillors were saloon owners, which I guess made regulation easy. It was also a city just like New York when it came to something else. You could pick up a guide to the brothels, human nature being constant it seems. They didn't play the numbers here but bet on horse racing, though I've never seen the sense in putting good money down on some dumb animal, though if things here were the same as back home, they doubtless had ways of taking the risk out of gambling.

It was a city, it appeared to me, then and in the days ahead, in a permanent churn. There were stores with their names in German, Italian, Hebrew. You could see Jewish peddlers on the passing street cars. Because of the fire, they had rebuilt in stone so there was a weight to it all. They were digging something called the Sanitary and Ship Canal, planning to reverse the flow of the Chicago River. What? Reverse a river? I could see why, though. When I turned a faucet on in the hotel, I saw small fish swimming around in the glass. I gather the water came from some pipe under the lake and people were used to feeling a tickle in the throat as something swam down inside them. When I showed her the glass she shrugged. It seemed that was how she communicated and so far nothing appeared to bother her. Still, it was another reason for drinking beer, but then there was always a reason for drinking beer.

You could smell the money in the air, though the local university had gone bankrupt, and that wasn't all you could smell. They were turning cattle and pigs into

meat in great buildings and at great speed. Speed
seemed to be what the city was about. What should I
have, then, but a steak when at last we found a place and
so, to my surprise, did she. She also took a beer. I was
beginning to revise my opinion of this woman. In fact, I
was beginning to think that this trip might prove more
interesting than I had thought. I had no idea, though,
how we would make our way out to South Dakota and
the idea of finding Sitting Bull seemed even more
ridiculous now I was half a continent away from the
man obsessed with Indians and believed they had the
key to the country.

'Aren't you nervous about this trip?'

'Why?'

'Well, you're a woman.'

She looked at me as though I were some kind of
fool. 'How many women do you think crossed the
continent? They raised children, fed them, looked after
them where no one had lived before, and you think I
should be nervous?'

This was clearly a line she thought worth repeating. 'Except for the Indians,' I added.

'I thought we were here to find Indians. You are worried about Indians you should have stayed in New York. I take pictures. I don't need someone who can only write words.'

'You think pictures trump words? This country was built on words, the Constitution, the Gettysburg address.'

'Words can lie. Pictures are what is.'

'Back home there are those off the boat who borrow a suit so those they left behind will think they are rich. Pictures are how people want to seem. Or what the person taking the picture wants them to look. Don't tell me you deal in truth.'

'And words aren't the same? Politicians lying themselves into office, reporters saying what they are told to say because those who own the papers have reasons why they want to keep things hidden or call people anarchists because it serves their purpose to do so.'

Well, that was something I hadn't expected. I had been paired with an anarchist and it was only four years since the Haymarket bomb here in Chicago. Then it was back to the hotel and a night on the couch before the next day meeting up with a man I was told would help. He worked for the *Tribune,* and naturally I met him in a bar. She stayed behind wanting to take some pictures, or so she said, though I suspect she might be checking out clothes, even as it was an open question whether men's or women's since she had already told me she aimed to disguise herself again when we moved on west.

I had been told that he knew his way around and could make arrangement for a consideration, the consideration being $20. He wasn't difficult to spot when he came in, dim though the light was. He had a small brown bowler perched on his head and striped railhead pants which would have looked fine on the vaudeville stage. He was smoking a large cigar and walked with a lurch like someone who had just come off a sailing ship. He had no difficulty seeing me because there were no more than a handful of men scattered

237

around, mostly on their own as if this were simply somewhere warm to be.

He sat down and extended a hand. It was cold and limp. 'How do you like Chicago?' he asked, breathing heavily, either out of breath from walking across the sawdust floor or suffering from asthma, which would not have been surprising given the cigar. 'Best city in America, the world,' he added, evidently happy to answer his own question. He leaned back, reached into his pocket and then sprinkled something on the end of the cigar. 'Opium,' he said, reading the question I was about to ask. And this was the man I had been told was dependable. 'A drink,' he said, not so much a question as a statement as he raised a hand and shouted 'whisky,' holding two fingers up, waving his wrist around. 'Find it cold?' he asked, then added 'lake weather.' I was beginning to wonder whether he needed anyone else or was content to conduct a dialogue with himself.

'So,' he said, once we had a glass in front of each of us.

'I need,' I began only for him to interrupt.

'Your health and welcome to the...'

'Best city in the world,' I suggested.

Evidently not being strong on irony, he nodded enthusiastically. 'Whisky,' he shouted again, sinking the one he already had. 'I'm from the *Tribune*,' he declared, as though I thought he might be a numbers man as from his appearance he might have been. 'Best newspaper,' he began before realising that I came from another one and might take offence. Instead, he said, 'My name's Charley, except to my mother, God bless her.'

Charley? Fritz, more likely since he spoke with a German accent and had probably abandoned his mother back in the homeland. I had already noticed that Chicago was another version of Berlin, there being so many Germans, at least those that were not Italian or Greek, this being a city much like my own especially when it came to those who thought hyperbole a true sign of citizenship. He cleared his throat, looked up at the ceiling, half reached into his pocket again and then said, 'there was, if you please, to be ...' He stopped, continuing to stare at the ceiling as though the proceedings no longer had any relevance to him.

'Ah,' I said, 'a consideration.'

He looked down with a broad smile on his face.

'Yes. A consideration my friend'

I could see he felt it necessary to get this piece of business over before going any further. Accordingly, I reached into my pocket and took out an envelope bearing the crest of the Palmer House Hotel. He watched as if this were maybe a magic trick and it would disappear. Once I had handed it over, though, he leaned back with a satisfied sound such as old people make when they sit down, before counting the bills. So much for trust, though if he was a newspaper man that gets stamped out of you pretty quick as people show a preference for lies when it comes to reporters.

'So?'

'I will make arrangements.'

'For what?'

'For you to go as you wish to this desolate place where only Indians live.'

'When? How?'

240

'A day. Two days. Maybe three.'

'Two,' I said. 'Meanwhile, I need a story or two.'

'There are stories. There are always stories.'

'What of Cronin?'

'Cronin? Yesterday's story.'

So it was, and we had covered it, but the smell was still in the air, and this was where it had ended, even if it started in my own tarnished city. It had everything, beginning with a secret Irish republican organisation aimed at throwing the British out of Ireland, an outcome much to the delight of those in the city's pubs. The Chicago police had had a hand in it, they being fluent in Irish nostalgia. The group had split, one of them turning out to be a British spy so that suspicion also fell on Patrick Cronin, a displaced leader who then ended up dead in a sewer, naked but for an Agnus Dei medallion, the protective power of the medal falling somewhat short of its advertised qualities. Now here was my territory, not chasing down Indians.

'All done'

'I know. One innocent, the others not. They're in the Joliet. But remember Lingg.'

He pulled a face, Louis Lingg having been German born but also a man who blew half his face off with a blasting cap in jail the day before his execution having been convicted of the Haymarket bomb, writing 'Hurrah for Anarchy' as he died. In German as I recall.

He caught my drift, this Gerhardt or Heinz or whoever he had been before Charley seemed the way to go.

'No bombs this time,' he said. 'For you, I am told, it is Sitting Bull. Yes? Cronin is finished. All done.'

Cases like that, though, never are. There are stories within stories and the game is to work your way down or out, whichever direction seems likely to lead somewhere. Then again, witnesses lie, juries are bribed, judges put their thumbs on scales that are supposed to balance, and word comes down from wherever word comes down from, saying enough is enough. End it. That's when it's time to look more closely. In this case, why the sewer? Why naked? Why the medal? Were the killers Catholic? And when you think of it, sewer, naked, medal, these were people who seemed to have taken care to set their stage, inviting such as me in.

The problem was I was a stranger in this city and whatever I had been told I already knew this man was not someone with his finger on the pulse working on a paper that was the greatest paper, in the greatest city, albeit with a certain tendency to set itself on fire, blow things and people up, drop the odd Irish conspiracist and possible spy into human effluent. I could only hope he was better at pointing us in the right direction.

As to Miss Bridie, she was full of herself having, she explained, been buying clothes at Marshall Fields on State Street before taking pictures of street railroads and the stock yards. She had been on the kill floor, watched them cut the hogs' throats, visited the soap works. Who was she? Which woman had I ever met who fancied passing her time seeing animals turned into soap? This was the woman who carried a gun and, who knows, maybe a grudge about men in general and me in particular.

'When are we going?' she asked.

'Good question. Two days, perhaps, though I was given a bill of goods when I was told the *Tribune* man was someone who would help.'

'Why do we need him?'

'Maybe we don't. A day or two and we'll know. Meanwhile, I need to think about writing something.'

'You should get to the stockyards.'

'You think the *Telegraph* readers need to know what happens there when they wash their faces or eat their steaks? Just the thing to read at breakfast.'

'Never turn away my father told me. If you do, you'll maybe miss what matters most, what others won't see, maybe don't want to see. True of those who take pictures. So, not true of people like you?'

'I've been in places you don't even know exist. Seeing is one thing. Rubbing other people's noses in what you see is another. You only take pictures. Freeze a moment. I have to tell a story, one moment leading to another.'

'Pictures are stories.'

This was an argument we would evidently keep having. She flicked her hair from her eyes, blue I realised, deep blue and, for a second, I could feel something more than irritation. Did her hair not have a shine? Was her smile, when she permitted, not compelling? No, this was a current I must resist, feeling, suddenly, an undertow, a quickening pulse. Then again, why not. Pictures and words come together after all, so maybe why not us. I had to fill my time with something on this mission to nowhere in particular for no reason I could detect.

'I'm hungry. I've got a list. There are Cheap Eats restaurants, but I fancy something more. How about the Lake House or Henrici's?'

'How about a bar? A five-cent beer will get you free food.'

She turned her blue eyes on me, and it was the Lake House. Somewhere along the line the idea of her as a man had disappeared, though I can't say she matched my idea of a woman either, what with her liking for guns and blood. Even so, it seemed that when she looked at me, she hesitated longer than she might before looking away. Perhaps here was a journey that might take me where I hadn't thought to go, which was alright with me since we were on a fool's errand, and the fool was sitting in a leather chair, with a cigar in his mouth, a thousand miles or more away.

What I had never realised, back in New York, where I was busy wondering how close to the truth I could get and still survive, was that it wasn't only my employer who was interested in Indians and Sitting Bull. The German hack had raised his eyebrows when I said I was looking for a story that interested no one. After all, this was Chicago that had been born from a meeting place where traders gathered, and traders would trade with the Devil if there was a percentage in it. And, for some, Indians were the Devil but, if they had skins to trade, well, why not sup with them. He smiled a lop-sides smile, but I could see how he thought I had got things wrong and I found out just how wrong when I read a piece in *The Dispatch* that said Buffalo Bill had had a dinner here with General A. 'Bear Coat' Miles at which he persuaded him to allow him to go and arrest the old Indian, though why he would choose to do that was hard to see since they were supposed to be friends or, given the way the world works, co-investors in lies about the frontier. It said how he had loaded a wagon with candy and set off. I could see how that might work on a bunch of children but why it would work on a warrior was hard to see. But what that principally meant to me was that a whole raft of newsmen would be setting out, no doubt with photographers less given to changing their sex than mine, to capture the drama. Which meant that we should be on our way. In truth, the papers were suddenly full of stories about Indians so that I realised we were late in the day. The point was to come up with stories others didn't have, even though the first thing you are taught to do is get hold of an early edition of the other papers and steal what you can. There were anyway those on those papers who for a dollar or two would let us know what might be coming.

It seems they had been dancing out there, thinking themselves bulletproof. Well, I knew a few back home who had treasured that illusion, not because they had some kind of miraculous shirt but because they were stupid and thought they were impervious when it came to a .22 slug from a Smith & Wesson Model 1, as Civil War soldiers thought themselves impenetrable to

Minié balls only for 600,000 plus to discover otherwise. Personally, I couldn't see what was wrong with a little dancing, though I recalled the Puritans called mixed dancing promiscuous and gynecandrical, which explains why they were against it. On the other hand, they were against almost everything, getting pleasure from stopping other people having any. I would have thought it gave us the edge if we were going up against Indians who thought they could run against Winchesters believing themselves immortal. But there you are. What did I know? Suddenly, though, even I was beginning to think there might be a story here and that maybe not only those in Chicago would have an interest. Buffalo Bill was the key, so it was time to be moving, though without the candy.

Even Miss Bridie got interested when she discovered that one of the reporters was a woman and photographers were shipping out, with or without guns, though I had begun to think that I should see what I could do to augment my pen and so got myself a Colt House Revolver.

It came in a fancy box along with a wooden tray to hold the bullets. It cost seventeen dollars, though whether that was a bargain or not I couldn't say. I was told it was the gun shot Boss Tweed's friend Diamond Jim Fisk, who had tried to corner the gold market, so if it was good enough to kill him it would no doubt serve whatever purpose I might have, though since I couldn't imagine any circumstance in which I would use it that was seventeen dollars I could have spent on eight or nine bottles of the finest whisky, even if it was not clear which might lead me in the direction of greater trouble. True, despite what I had said to her, I did have a gun back in my New York home, a Colt .45, but having purchased it from a man in a bar I discovered it faulty so that it was as well I had never ventured with it when I planned to meet with those who might have been impressed but probably would not have been having weapons of their own and being practiced with them.

There were women reporters in New York, but, with the one exception, they were mostly interested in calling for garbage to be collected or explaining where you could buy clothes to impress men, though I never knew a man who could give a fig what women wore being more concerned with taking off whatever they had spent so long putting on. There was Jennie June. She wrote on fashion and anyway came from England where such things might seem normal. Then I recalled there was Jane Swisshelm who had wanted Indians killed out in Minnesota or some other godforsaken place, but she was dead. I don't know about the Indians; except I seem to remember they were Sioux like the ghost dancers so may not have taken delivery of the bullet proof shirts in time. None of the women reporters, would have ventured out here, though Nellie Bly might have done.

We needed to get to Standing Rock, which was no more than a name on a map, but it turned out we could go some distance by railroad, which hardly seemed likely, but there you are. There were railroads like a spider's webs, the spider being Chicago. Companies owned the land alongside the tracks and a station meant maybe a town and therefore money to be made. Railroads were money on wheels, those that weren't phantoms designed to bamboozle investors where not a single rail was laid.

Even I knew that it was the railroads that killed off more Indians than the cavalry. No wonder they hated them. They lived off the buffalo, but white men slaughtered them for the fun of it. They didn't call him

Buffalo Bill for nothing. He killed as many as he could, but not a patch on what happened later. There is a thing about my countrymen and guns. There's nothing quite like killing one of God's creatures, especially if they are big enough for someone with eyeglasses half an inch thick to hit. Mind you, in my closet I've got a coat with a mildewed buffalo fur collar which I wear when I don't care what I look like, nor the smell that never quite disappears.

I had never given much thought to railroads or Indians before, or the great nothing which makes up the something we like to call our country. Who cared about some bunch of people who couldn't read the *Telegraph* if you gave it to them free and spent one half of their life painting themselves red and the other half slaughtering one another or, for preference, any white people crazy enough to think farming in the great American desert a good idea, though before Sitting Bull decided to let himself be spat at in an arena. I recall how he had carried a flag at the opening of the Northern Pacific. So, that's how much he hated the railroads. There had been a piece in the *Sun* that said he looked like a backwoods

Methodist bishop, so it turned out I remembered more than I had thought about the Chief.

Back in '83, when the last spike was hammered in by the Northern Pacific Railroad to celebrate the conclusion of the transcontinental railroad, who should they ask to be there but Sitting Bull himself. The papers were full of his speech, and they must have thought they had finally enrolled him in whatever cause they thought they were serving. But I heard that the translation read out was different from what he said in Sioux, which was an outright attack on whites. I don't know if that was true, but it must have been near enough because I learned there were those whose careers were blighted as a result. Why would they have thought it a good idea to get him to celebrate something that joined up the Atlantic and Pacific as if we owned the whole land in between and he was no more than a prop in a national pageant? I like to think it was true, not because I carried any sort of torch for those who had slaughtered whole families but because I recognised flimflam when I saw it. It certainly said something for him who had fooled them into thinking he was tamed when he was only fighting in a different way.

Strangely, I gather it was this that had led to an invitation to appear in the Wild West Show, which makes you wonder what he was up to. Apparently, they were happy to get rid of him at the Agency, but I suspect it had been his way of keeping himself at the middle of things. That show seemed to celebrate his defeat when I suspect it was another way of winning. Did it not occur to anyone that he had plans of his own? Well, it didn't to me, not having any interest in him. And if I got to talk to him, what would he say? He had caught people out once, why not again.

Meanwhile, if you think love bloomed on that journey, think again. Trains may be the only way to travel but you end up with grit in your eyes, dirt round your cuffs, and a conversation which runs into the sand, not that we talked all that much. I was trying to write up a story about my visit to Joliet prison where I had had a word with Martin Burke, convicted for murdering Cronin and who seemed more indignant about being captured in Canada than he was about being found guilty, even as he insisted he was innocent. I suspect he had reasons for thinking there were those who would find ways to get him out, though quite why was beyond me.

So, Chicago had not been a total waste. I had already telegraphed a piece. I got a two-word reply: INDIANS STOP, which you could read in a number of ways, but I knew what it meant and who had it sent. And they didn't waste money when it came to using the telegraph. On the other hand, I had some friends who weren't on salary and wrote pieces where they were paid by the word. They would send in stories saying, 'FIERCE STORM IN KANSAS CITY. THUNDER GOES BANG BANG BANG BANG BANG.'

CHAPTER FOURTEEN: ANOTHER SECRET REVEALED

I say it would be wrong to think that love
bloomed in the desert lands, but that is not to say that
we didn't both feel the need for a little comfort,
especially when I broke out the whisky I had bought in a
store which specialised in intoxicants as judged not only
by its full shelves but also by those resting in the gutter
outside having wasted no time in discussing the varying
virtues of alcohol on offer for a variety of prices,
including those they could afford no matter it might turn
them blind. It transpired that she was as accomplished a
drinker as me, though both of us slid together into that
state in which reason is set aside, along with inhibitions,
taste, blind common sense. The next day neither of us
could look at one another or, in my case, even
remember things too clearly so that perhaps I dreamed it
all, more especially since she had now taken to dressing
as a man again. That thought alone made me hope I had
stopped short of anything that might stay with me in
years to come.

255

It happened, or perhaps didn't, in another of those nowhere places that had an idea that it might one day become a somewhere. The engine had broken down, this evidently being common enough. It struck me as odd that it chose to come to a halt just as we were pulling into what passed as a station in what passed as a town in what passed as a territory. Perhaps there was some kind of agreement with whoever owned the half-finished building that had a sign on it saying 'HOTEL,' though I took this for western humour since there was nothing about it that justified that word. And in truth the last two letters were displaced so that doubtless in the summer months it spoke a truth which it did not in winter. There was a bar, though, so that I was inclined to give it the benefit of the doubt. No one said anything about my drinking companion since they were mostly doing what we were, namely drinking to remember to forget, which is also how come I was later somewhat hazy about what followed.

Where was this? I'd like to say I knew but out there one place looked much like another. I am pretty good at directions, though that is because where I come from there are street signs and uptown is one way and downtown is the other. There's the East River and the Hudson and that's about all you need to know. Out here I couldn't say for sure where I was beyond on my way to some other place that at least had a name.

And that's pretty much how it went, except it got colder and the point of it all began to get ever less clear though there was a story after all or why would others have been chasing it. That's the way with stories. One minute no one cares or knows anything, while the next you are climbing over each other to get there first. That's the newsman's motto. Be there first. And if you can't be there first, steal from those who are.

I'd noticed something, though. While part of me thought this was the very kind of place I had escaped from, there was something about it. In the day the sky was wide, reaching down to the land as it didn't in the city. And the nights, when I lay awake, were a maze of crystals scattered across black velvet. God knows how distant the stars are or why they were there at all, but they spoke to some mystery that would never be penetrated. As the train moved on, toward whatever fate lay in store, I watched the way the moon painted the world in silver. This was a place where time seemed suspended, and I could understand why the Indians treated it as sacred. Nothing sacred about the Bowery, no silver dusting on Broadway except nickels and dimes dropped by drunks. And the air was different. Not on the train, where it was the tart taste of steam and smoke swirling by. Outside, though, it was clean, no stink of horse shit, no smell of cooking sausages or knishes. Mind you, I could have done with some of the oysters and clams you could buy from street vendors along Broadway.

The wind here could cut to the quick, with nothing to stop it for a thousand miles, but I knew from my youth that it could gentle the unrelenting heat of summer, a blessing to those lying in tangled sheets where water from the well could go tepid in carrying it to the kitchen. Travelling does something. You leave more than a place behind. It is as though you step back from yourself and everything you thought you knew seems less important. Perhaps it was this place, far from anything, not yet tamed, marked out, owned, or perhaps it was a man who had become a woman and who, whatever I said to myself, had begun to seem necessary.

When she fell asleep, I watched her face, relaxed, beautiful, yes, beautiful though that was a word that seemed out of place given that I still had a hard time forgetting her other identity. And what did I really know of her? She was deception on deception. Perhaps that was part of the attraction. All I knew was that something had happened to me that I wasn't ready to admit, still less understand. Again, maybe it was because we were so far away from a place where I thought I understood who people were and, knowing that, kept myself secure from feeling anything but suspicion. It went with my trade. Yet here I was, deceived, yet compelled. Then there was a sudden jolt, and I was back on a train, watching a woman wake up and look around, a dream quickly dissolving. After a second, she looked at me and smiled and I felt as I did when looking down from the bridge a thousand miles away, feeling how easy it would be to let go and fall into the waiting water.

Not long before we reached the end of the line, an Indian got on. I don't know why that seemed strange, except I expected them to be off fighting the army, riding bareback or carrying babies on their backs. He sat down and stared ahead, his hair cut short and wearing a jacket somehow caught between two versions of himself. Then he opened a small case and took out a book and damn me if it wasn't a Bible. Someone had obviously done a job on him. Perhaps those men back in Boston who had translated one that no one would ever be able to read. Next, he took out a knife and I wondered whether he was an Old Testament or New Testament Indian, preferring vengeance over love. In the end he used it to cut some black whatever and thrust it in his mouth. He saw me watching and leant forward though, as it turned out, not to remove my scalp but offer me some of the black whatever, thrusting it forward along with the knife. I couldn't figure whether accepting or refusing was more likely to prompt an attack when once again my partner astonished me holding out her hand and accepting what was offered on the tip of the knife. She nodded. He nodded. I tried a smile, though it wouldn't come. So, we travelled on, both of them chewing while I looked out at the nothing that was flying past, a few flakes of snow now mixing in with the smoke and the sparks, heat and cold brought together like some metaphor whose meaning escaped me.

Eventually, we made it to Standing Rock. We were there to meet Sitting Bull, though why he would want to meet us was beyond me. And truth to tell he didn't. By then, though, I had done my homework and wasn't going to listen to some aborigine say no. Most of the people I interview would prefer I didn't unless they have something to sell, which in the end most do, so no is not a word I am willing to hear. You have to give them a reason, even if it is not one they would have thought of themselves. In the end everyone has a story and what is the point of a story if you keep it to yourself, though when they read it in the paper they are unlikely to recognise it. The story in your head seldom matches the one that appears in print. But who is to say if my version isn't truer than theirs?

The thing about newspapers is that while they have a lifespan equivalent to that of the mayfly, which is born, mates and dies in a single day, offering us a glimpse of our own tenure on the earth, they get stored away and I had spent some hours trying to learn something about him from what my fellow journalists had chosen to present as the truth. It wasn't good. I knew about Little Big Horn and the blond hero Custer whipped by a band of Indians who never went to West Point or dressed for dinner. What I hadn't realised was how the papers couldn't make up their minds whether Sitting Bull was a savage with blood dripping out of his mouth or some redskin statesman. Some said he was short as Napoleon and fluent in French. Others had him tall and illiterate. If you've read a book called *Moby Dick*, and, like my companion, you won't have done because nobody I ever met has, there is a white whale in that, and it seems to mean whatever people want it to mean. Incidentally, don't waste your time. It is interminable or, would be if I had finished it. It tells you everything you never wanted to know about the whaling industry which I can assure you is of no interest to anyone. Nonetheless, Sitting Bull is the white whale, only red. He is evidently anything anyone wants him to be. I've read my Cooper, whose hero keeps changing his name along with his clothes. He couldn't make his mind up either. One moment his Indians were drunk as a skunk, the next princes of the prairies.

I'm not sure there is a single thing I learned about Sitting Bull that is true. Whatever he had been in the past, he wasn't any more. In fact, it turned out he had become a farmer and was more concerned with the state of his corn than capturing white women and turning them into squaws, not that he ever did that or many of the things he was supposed to have done.

On the other hand, I quickly learned that things had changed with the dancing. To me, it hardly mattered if they wanted to spend their time prancing around except that was only a part of it and I could see how telling the dancers that a messiah was coming and that the white man would disappear wasn't likely to be to the taste of politicians in Washington or those who had been sold on the idea that they stood for progress and that things were theirs to take if they only went west. And I had read how the reservation of the Sioux had been sliced up and part of it sold off. On the other hand, what was wrong with that? Did the Indians represent the future? Not unless your idea of that was people looking for buffalo which had long since been shipped back east as bones and fur.

To my surprise we did get to meet James McLaughlin, in charge of the Agency. The surprise was that he let it be known that he regarded newspapermen as troublemakers, news of the supposed Messiah putting pressure on him from Washington. Since he had agreed to an interview, or at least to talking, the word interview clearly bothering him, doubtless he expected to be able to bend any story in his direction, which is the mistake made by many who talk when they should probably remain silent. To my even greater surprise he was married to a woman from what someone told me was a tribe who were a kind of Sioux, who went by a name which I could barely spell, though there was Irish and French in there somewhere, which was odd since he was in charge of all the Sioux on the reservation. Someone else told me she was a half-breed Santee from South Carolina, but I had no idea which was right. I was still trying to recover from the news that the man in front of me, put in charge of the Sioux, was actually married to one of them.

He looked like a banker with silver hair and moustache. Yet he told me he had ridden with the Indians on a buffalo hunt eight years before when there were fifty thousand of the animals nearby, they killing a tenth of them and he a few on his own. It was hard to reconcile with the man I now saw. In truth, though, I had no interest in his exploits, true or not, though who cannot believe a man who looks like a banker. Well, me for a start having written an article or two about the vultures in neat suits and top hats who squatted in buildings with Grecian columns while they became richer by making others poorer.

'They carried off the meat' he explained, his eyes bright, 'while others were jerking it and making pemmican.'

He might as well have been speaking French for all I understood what jerking and pemmican might mean.

'They were Hunkpapas, Black Feet, Upper and Lower Yanktonais.'

Really. I was back with *Moby Dick* and everything I didn't want to know about whales. Now it was Indians.

'I'll never forget that time.'

Right. I could just see readers in Brooklyn wanting to know all about the Hunkpapas who sounded more like a bunch of German fathers than some Indian tribe slaughtering animals. He no doubt saw my scepticism for he now told me that the Hunkpapa Sioux had been at the Little Big Horn, which, he insisted, the Indians for some reason called Greasy Grass, not entirely grasping the essence of newspapers which is that they don't tell yesterday's stories. And if they did, I couldn't imagine that a tale of the Battle of Greasy Grass would have sold many papers. Besides, John Finnerty of the *Chicago Times* had got that story at the time, along with Kellogg of the *New York Herald* a decade and a half back.

'Sitting Bull' I began.

'He was a coward. Where was he during the fight? Not there. He was just camped nearby. It was Chief Bull in command. Along with Crazy Horse. They weren't looking for a fight. They had their families with them. What Sitting Bull did was prophesy a defeat for the whites near the Big Horn River. Turned out he was right.'

'Crazy Horse. How the hell did someone get a name like that?'

He ignored me. 'It was all about opening the Black Hills for mining. Gold fever. Never mind the treaty.'

So, he was an Indian lover. I don't know what I had expected but hardly a man who hunted buffalo with the Indians and stood up for them against progress, if digging gold could be said to be that.

'About Sitting Bull,' I began. 'The dancing stuff.'

'You must understand something. He is ambitious, crafty, and avaricious. He is not a chief and I find no redeeming qualities in him. On the other hand, he is powerful, smart, and his medicine is good.'

'His medicine?'

'Little Big Horn.'

A strange kind of medicine it seemed to me.

'I met him when he was a prisoner. He was on the steamer General Sherman when I first came here.'

Some people have stories they want to tell whether you have the slightest interest or not, and you have to hear them out if you are going to get at what you actually want to know. Even so, I wasn't ready for his life story.

'My job here was to make sure he made no mischief, which I did until Kicking Bear came along.'

'Kicking Bear?'

'From the Cheyenne reservation. He's a Miniconjou. Bringing news of the Messiah. He was here some weeks back. Crazy.'

'Right. So that would be different from the Messiah white people look for.'

'Absolutely different. Though they thought it the same. He told him that Christ had appeared but that he wasn't white.'

'Not white? But didn't Christ live where pretty well nobody was white?

'Of course he was white, but according to Kicking Bear he was an Indian. And why had he come at all? To tell them to dance. That's how stupid this is.'

'So, no feeding of the five thousand or turning water into wine.'

'He was wearing moccasins, for God's sake. Can you imagine Christ wearing moccasins? And he danced. The Son of God danced. This is what he came to tell Sitting Bull'

Truth to tell, I had a hard time imagining him at all. He looked at me suspiciously not realising that I had always regarded religion as a confidence trick. The more impossible a thing was the more people believed, feeling guilty, not to say afraid, if they didn't sign up to any nonsense. Dancing seemed pretty tame beside smiting people, turning wives into salt, and sacrificing children to show you would do anything if word came down from above. It always seemed to me that everyone in this country is crazy, except they are crazy in different ways and at different times. Maybe that's our saving grace. And gullible besides.

'He told Sitting Bull he had been taken up into the clouds and shown all the land, a land without white men and full of buffalo.'

Full of something to do with buffalo, certainly.

'The white men would be buried under the soil, and they would lose the ability to make gunpowder so that no Indians could be harmed. They only had to dance. That was the message Kicking Bear brought and Sitting Bull saw it as giving him back the authority he lost when he had fled to Canada, was arrested and imprisoned.' He smiled as if he had just been retrieving the ravings of a madman, as perhaps he was. 'Which is why we have to move against him.'

'If you arrested people for believing what some preacher said then most of the country would be in prison.' He ignored me. 'Are you religious?'

'Catholic.'

'Don't you have ceremonies, singing, parading around, carrying good luck charms though you call them something different? Don't you believe in a Second Coming, that there are rewards for those who believe? Is that so different?'

'We don't wear shirts that we say are bullet proof.'

'But you do believe that the dead will rise again.'

I could see this wasn't going down too well.

'We offer them the blessings of the Church. Ours is a religion of peace.'

This wasn't the moment to remind him that the Bible had been carried by both sides a quarter of a century earlier when we were busy slaughtering one another because we came from different parts of the country, took a different view on states' rights, slavery. But in my experience people will convince themselves of anything if it serves their purpose. Anyway, he clearly wasn't interested in debating religion, anymore, I confess, than was I, he being anxious to get back to the subject in hand, which was Sitting Bull.

'I ordered that Kicking Bear should be sent back to his reservation, but Sitting Bull broke his peace pipe in front of the ghost dancers so that I knew I would have to act. I recommended he should be arrested and moved to prison. I'd done that before, but the military had the ultimate say.'

'For dancing?'

'You're from the East. It's a different world out here.'

There was no denying that. After all, evidently this was where government officials talked about ghosts, rode with Indians killing buffalo, embraced some Indians while denouncing others and even married one.

'There's no risk of an outbreak here. I said as much to the Department. We've only got to arrest a few troublemakers. Along with Sitting Bull, Circling Bear and Black Bird.'

Why not the whole menagerie? Jumping Weasel, Arthritic Toad?

'It was Sitting Bull who caused all the trouble a year ago. They were offered a fair price for their land. Most signed. We needed three-fourths.'

'So, he didn't sign?'

'We didn't need him. I used someone else. Wrote his speech for him. It was in the papers. I thought you were a newspaperman. Don't you read your own papers?'

Mostly not, was the true answer. I certainly wouldn't have been interested in a bunch of Indians selling their land in some godawful part of the country where I assumed there was nothing much more than an occasional snake and the US Army riding around looking for somewhere they could lose to those same Indians again. Now if it had been in Brooklyn or, more likely, Manhattan much above 40th Street, then I would have noticed alright mostly because I would have assumed that someone had a finger in the pie.

'And the press hasn't helped with stories about the Messiah and dancing. Would that be why you are here?'

'Truth to tell I'm here because my editor does what his proprietor tells him to, and I do what my editor tells me to do. I don't deal in religion, buffalos, medicine men. I was sent to interview Sitting Bull, so that's what I have to do.'

'You've been sent on a fool's errand then, my friend. He won't speak to you. He speaks through Bull

Ghost, known as One-Eyed Riley having only one eye. Besides, I'm about to order his arrest. And what is the man doing you came with?'

One-eyed Riley. Now I had heard everything. 'Who knows. He's a bundle of surprises. No doubt he is wandering around taking pictures. At least I hope he is since that is the only reason he came along.'

'Well, at least he speaks the language.'

'The language? Which language?'

'Sioux. Lakota Sioux.'

'What? He doesn't speak Sioux. He's from New York. We don't speak Sioux there. We barely speak English.'

He shrugged. First, she was a man, then a woman, then a man again and now had become a squaw.

'They dance around a sacred pole, chanting as they go and when one collapses Sitting Bull pretends they whisper messages in his ear which he then says are coming from the dead. Then he tells them to take vapor-baths each morning, closed in a wickiup with water poured over heated rocks. I went to reason with him, but he refused to hear though I had done him many favours over the years. Hence, we are come to where we are today.'

It occurred to me that there were people in Manhattan who paid good money to be sweated in a box, if that is what it was, and I have been in theatres where performers hear messages from the departed who evidently haven't departed far enough not to be heard.

'If you are to arrest him, I would like to be a witness.'

'And what would you write?'

'Only what I see.'

'In my experience people see what they will. Besides, there will be nothing to see. The Indian police will do their duty and the whole will be over in minutes.'

'Is there time for me to speak to him?'

'I told you, he is not going to want to talk to anyone. Especially someone from the East.'

'You forget. He was in the Wild West Show.'

'I can hardly forget. Colonel Cody was here, sent by General Miles. Happily, he was turned away at my request or there would have been trouble.'

So that was why the reporters had gone away, because I had seen none of them since arriving. 'Have you talked to him?'

'Sitting Bull? Certainly, I've talked to him. I don't think he believes any of it. Doesn't dance himself. Said he wouldn't. That was it. He wrote me a letter saying they prayed to God just like us, only a different God. Said he knew I didn't like him, which is true enough, and that he had been told I was going to see that all his ponies and guns were taken away, which is not true. He was determined to go to Pine Ridge.'

'If he's not dancing surely the whole thing will just wear out unless you expect the Messiah to put in an appearance.'

'You're right. It will end. But cut him out and we can get on with the business of educating them.'

'Educating?'

276

'Americanising. You think they have a future unless they change? I've seen them change. One day we won't even think of them as Indians.'

Well, that will go down well with them, I thought. On the whole I couldn't give a damn either way except you don't take land away from Americans. You don't corral them like wild horses, and you don't make them line up for food. But what do I know not having any land to take away, living in an apartment with others above, below and beside me. True, I don't get given food. I have to work for it, but I don't get much choice what it is I do. I'm not ordered around by someone given charge of a reservation. I'm ordered around by a man who no one ever voted for. If someone told me that if I danced, it would all go away I'd put my dancing shoes on right away.

It was then that he/she came in. 'Say something,' I said.

'Say what?'

'Say something in Sioux.'

She looked across at McLaughlin.

'He's agreed,' she said.

'Who?'

'Sitting Bull.'

'You've spoken to him?'

'Someone who spoke for his son.'

'What's he like?'

'He hates us.'

'Well, that's a good start. You are supposed to be taking pictures.'

'I have.'

'Not a good idea,' said McLaughlin.

'What's the harm?'

'I could refuse permission.'

'Yes. That would look good in the *Telegraph*. There are those back East who still think of him riding round the arena and signing autographs.'

'He's a pernicious influence, him and his band along the Grand River.'

'Are you afraid of violence, then?'

'Not at all. The Indian police will do the job.'

'And the military?'

'Not to be involved.'

'So, there is no harm in our watching.'

'And what will you write? My orders came down from the President.'

'Directly?'

'I have no need of stories that stir up trouble.'

'You said there will be none.'

'Nor there will, but not everyone understands what this man is like. Believe me, once he has been removed, we can get on with the country's business.'

'Which is?'

'Progress, my friend, progress.'

'And the Indians?'

'Good Christian Americans. He doesn't even believe in what he is doing. He is an old man trying to cling on to power.'

'Pretty American already, then.'

Afterwards we sat where they had chosen to put us, in a small cabin which looked out over a square where Indians were being taught to be Americans by having their hair cut, wearing Sunday school clothes, and being taught to farm where nothing grows, especially given that earlier in the year I was told everything had been burned away by the sun. Once on our own she had changed into a woman again, which was no less disturbing for me now than it had been before.

'So,' I said when we were sat down at last, 'how come you speak Sioux?'

'My mother.'

'Your mother?'

' I told you I have another name. Winona.'

'What does it mean?'

'What does John mean. It's a name. It means first born daughter.'

'What tribe?'

For a moment I thought she wouldn't reply, then she said, 'Sioux,' as though I should have realised, which, of course, I should have done. How else would she speak the language?

'How on earth … what … where …' I didn't quite know how to get into it.

'My own business.'

'Why didn't you …'

'What's it to do with you? Why do you think I pushed for this assignment?'

'I thought you were … I thought someone …'

'Yes? I heard about it and made myself available.'

'But why?'

'Because nobody gives a shit about them. Every treaty we made with them …'

So, them. And we. At least she hadn't forgotten who she was.

'Every treaty was broken. If we couldn't wipe them out – and we tried, God we tried – then we would transform them into us destroying who they were, who they are.'

'Progress.' I was echoing McLaughlin, but it was clear enough, surely.

'Progress? Progress?' She half turned away from me as though that was all she needed to say.

'You think they could go on being the way they were. No buffalo. The army. People streaming in. Things are moving on. You think they could stay the way they were, where they were?'

She swung around. 'We tell them where they can live. When someone wants their land, we push them off. Meanwhile, we sweep on by in search of what exactly? We laugh at their names, what they believe in, everything that matters to them that doesn't to us. We don't even know how many different tribes there are. Did you think all Sioux are the same? They're not.'

It was quite a speech but meant nothing at all even if the same thoughts had occurred to me. Things were as they were and there was no percentage in trying to change them. She was right, though. I didn't know a thing beyond what I had read in Washington and though that had made me think, thinking was where it stopped. She took herself into another room.

'When are we seeing him?' I called.

There was silence and then she hissed, 'when we get there. He's not here. Just a man who speaks for him. And I am translating.'

'He speaks English.'

'What he says in English is not what he thinks in Sioux.'

'And is that true of you?' Then a thought occurred. 'Where is your mother.'

She reappeared and glared at me, her eyes narrowing. 'Dead.'

What should I say but ,'I'm sorry.'

'Sorry?'

283

'How did she …?'

She turned away again, and I thought I heard a sob. Then she went back into the other room, slamming the door behind her.

I called after her. 'What about the woman?' There was a pause and then she opened the door a touch.

'What woman?'

'Catherine Weldon.'

'What of her?'

'I heard she made a pitch for him, or the other way around. She came from Brooklyn.'

That was all I could remember, beyond the fact that a man on McLaughlin's staff had said they might have been married. At least she had stayed in his cabin along with his Indian wives, and he had had nine of those. Nine. But it obviously touched a nerve.

'Are you crazy? She shipped back east.'

'Yes, but why? Is there a story here?'

'If there was it has already been told and nobody believed it except someone like you more used to pork-barrelling politicians than people who want to help. Especially women.'

'I guess he spoke English to her, unless they learn Sioux in Brooklyn,' which seemed a smart thing to say except that she herself had learned to speak it wherever it was she came from. Not Tombstone.

Later, when she had calmed down, I asked again about her mother. You don't get to be a reporter by taking no for an answer.

'Where did they meet, your father and mother?'

She looked at me and I could see how she was wondering whether to walk away again. There was something in her eyes. Something in me, too. I had tried to push it away but there was no denying I felt something. Every time she changed into a woman I felt the ground shift beneath my feet. Well, I would, given that she was one thing one moment and something else the next, but it was more than that and I guess I knew it, had since that moment we had both chosen to forget but which I certainly could not. Yet there was a barrier there, alright. Was it coldness? Fear? No, not that. She didn't seem to fear anything unless it was someone who wanted to get close to her and, against all my instincts, and a lifetime of moving on, of relationships that went nowhere, I was beginning to feel that I wanted precisely that. Sometimes private issues trump public ones. Actually, always in my experience. Who cares, in the end, about Indians and graft and careers when what matters is some other person who has broken through defences you never knew you had put in place. On the other hand, I have thought that once or twice in the past and ended up thinking career more important not least because what is born in an evening can dissolve with the dawn. Even a month or so is no protection. So, what to do now except not accept the risk.

I got out the whisky and poured us both a glass, a full glass. I had half a dozen other bottles in my valise. There'd been no point in taking a chance. I held it out to her. She looked at it and then at me. She knew what I was up to, but she took it anyway. She sat down and looked across at the window. Clouds had gathered and it looked as though the weather would break.

'He was army,' she said, leaning back.

'He?'

'My father. Cavalry.'

'I thought he took photographs.'

'That was later.'

I took a drink, leaving it to her. She took a drink herself and I could see where she was wondering whether to stop there. There was a roll of thunder outside, though I had never noticed the lightning.

'There was no fighting then. He met her on the reservation. She had been married. He had been killed on a raid. There were settlers. Chose the wrong place, the wrong moment. A patrol came across them and he was shot. That had been a year before. He should have been the enemy and was, I suppose. I don't know what happened but when my father went back east, she was with him.'

'So that's ...'

'I was born.'

'She spoke English?'

'Some.'

287

'So you …'

'Both.'

'Was it …?'

'What do you think, a white man married to an Indian? And how do you think people treated me. Even those rescued were treated like dirt. Me? I was seen as the spawn of the Devil, except she died. Another child. Dead like her.'

'How old …'

'Eighteen.'

'What was she …'

'She was my mother.'

'And your father.'

'Ashamed. Nobody made it easy.'

I could imagine. 'Where were you living?'

'All over. I told you, he was Cavalry. You think an Indian for a wife made him popular, though there were plenty kept one. Handy when you are away from home. He drank. Maybe that's where I got the taste. There was another reason, though.'

She took a long drink. There was another rumble of thunder. I'd been told there had been a drought until Sitting Bull called down the rain. I could see how the drink had got to her, or our being out here away from everything we knew, everything I knew, at least.

'There was something else.'

I don't think she was really talking to me. Certainly, she was gazing off somewhere, the window suddenly lit up with a flash of lightning.

'Who'd you think scalped her husband?'

'Some other Indian?' I knew the tribes spent as much time fighting each other as soldiers.

'My father did. It was what they did.'

'The soldiers did? Did she know?'

'That's why she tried to kill him.'

This was getting stranger by the moment.

'She tried to kill your father?'

'Not until the end. I think he understood. That was why she killed my brother and herself. She failed to kill my father, so she did what I guess she felt she had to do.'

She was silent, and so was I. What do you say when you're told something like that? And who was the savage? Out here was where savagery was supposed to come up against civilisation. That was what the frontier was all about, yet both sides seemed as bad as one another.

'What did your father do?'

'Oh, he killed himself,' she said, her voice flat, the thunder shaking the room. 'Shot himself. I've still got his gun. He left it in his will. I tried to follow them but as you see decided against it.'

I didn't really know what to say. None of this matched up to the person I saw before me, the woman who had faced down men who thought to steal from her.

'He taught me things, though.'

'What things?'

'About guns. And what they could do.'

'That was it?'

'No. He taught me nothing is what it seems and in the end, nobody knows what they will do.'

'And the photography?'

'He had done some of that. He left me his equipment, too.'

'That's all he left you?'

'You mean besides his body in the outhouse? When I went through his things I came across a box and inside it was a dried-up scalp. He had kept it, you see. You're trying to figure me out. I wish you luck. I've tried that myself and had no success. But I have learned to fend for myself. And I have learned something along the way, and I don't mean about taking photographs. I've learned how mostly what we are told is wrong. I've learned how people keep secrets and I've learned not to trust anybody.'

She finished her whisky and held the glass out for more. And I thought I was damaged, thought my family was an excuse for who I was and had become. Well, I couldn't compete with her, but it was one more reminder that most people are pretty messed up and that cruelty is never far away. 'How come you don't look like one?'

'One what?'

'Indian. You don't look like one.'

'It happens.'

'I've never seen it.'

'How do you know? There are black people pass as white. Would you know them? You pass as a journalist. Who knew?'

'Smart. So, what do you want to be?'

'When I've grown up, you mean? I guess I want to be myself.'

'What if you don't like that self,' I asked, a question I have asked myself more than once.

'Is that all the whisky you've got?' she asked, the room growing brighter as the storm passed.

It wasn't, of course. Why on earth would it be? I went to my valise and took out another bottle, glad I had taken precautions back in Chicago, though I nearly made the mistake of going into Evanston until someone told it was dry. Anyway, it was that second bottle that led us to make that same mistake again, me waking to find her staring at me as though I had crept up on her in the night. She was dressed. What had we done? Well, I knew what we had done; it was the meaning of it foxed me as it did her given the expression on her face. I couldn't make out if it was puzzlement or as if she had just found a brown spider in her shoes. We neither of us spoke. These things happen. It wasn't the first time a few drinks, quite a few drinks, had led to something I would rather not put a word to. This, though, wasn't like those times, though I wasn't ready to say why. She shrugged. What did that mean? Just one of those things? Let's forget it? Then she shook her head, and that was it. She got up and left. As for me, I just lay there not knowing what I felt.

CHAPTER FIFTEEN: SITTING BULL

There are moments that twist you about, and this was one of them. Just when you think you have things figured out it turns out you haven't. Perhaps it was her fault. She was a shape shifter, or maybe that was the thing that drew me, never quite knowing who she was and what she was thinking. The Indian bit, though, was something else. Was that just a story she told to appear more interesting? Maybe I just like puzzles. Why else did I like figuring out who is stealing from whom, who was doing what to who and why? All the same, I couldn't get her out of my head though for all we had done what we had done I still couldn't figure out what it meant, if it meant anything beyond the fact that drink can make you do things you didn't think you would.

Then word came down that Sitting Bull had decided against talking to us, even if one of us was part Sioux. No reason given. Maybe he didn't like the idea of a woman if he had been told that was what she was, though I would like to have been there when she drew back the curtain. Or maybe he had heard about what she found in her father's box. That left me with a problem since that was the whole reason of my coming here. What was I to say once I got back to the *Telegraph*? I could already imagine getting a summons from the man upstairs, this being the second time I had failed to get a story about Indians who were supposed to hold the answer to the meaning of America.

There was nothing for it but to go back to McLaughlin to see what I could rescue. He had talked about arresting Sitting Bull. Maybe we could go along. That would give me something. And maybe she could take a picture or two. Anyway, stories are what you choose to make them. I suppose it was historic in a way. The man who had been at Little Big Horn, who had escaped to Canada, been part of a show, danced a dance, arrested like a common criminal. The end of a dream? Revenge? A final victory? Which page would it be on? Well, given the money they had spent on bringing me here with a man who was a woman, a white woman who was an Indian, probably page one. There was a story in her but that wasn't one we could run. It would give Fickey a heart attack. If the *World* ever found out it

would be even worse. I can just imagine Dana getting
word of it. It would maybe even give Pulitzer a laugh
and certainly readers in Queens. How come Fickey let
her sign up for all this without checking unless word
had come down from upstairs as it must have done?
And if it did how would a man who rarely ventured out,
and who I couldn't imagine ever knowing anything
about women, know she even existed let alone that she
was what she was. No, something had gone on that I
couldn't fathom, so there was no point in trying.

Finally, we got the word. McLaughlin was
determined to head off the military and use his own
Indian police. The very idea of Indian police seemed
odd to me. Why would Indians sign up to become police
in the first place, wearing a unform and carrying a metal
badge? Back where I came from there were those who
were overcome with shame if their sons joined what
they thought of as the enemy, unless they saw a
percentage in it. But here were those who had chased
buffalo, waged war, did everything to stop us civilising
them, happy to arrest their own kind. But there had
always been those who acted as scouts, tracking for the
army.

I still couldn't understand why anyone should care if Sitting Bull had now taken to dancing. As far as I could see none of them were going on the warpath and there were plenty of people who believed wilder things than them. Leaving them alone seemed the best thing, but I guess there were those who never forgot the Little Big Horn or the fact that he was not like them and could therefore be treated as they wished.

I read how people rode west seeking out famous gunfighters so they could go up against them. Whether they lived or died their name would always be tied to the man they faced on some dusty road while others watched, wagering on who would be dropped and who survive. Maybe taking Sitting Bull down was much the same.

We had been told the arrest would take place the following week but suddenly things had changed. It seems word had come that the messiah was about to appear at Pine Ridge, which would be worth the front page if he did. Maybe I could interview him. "Say, good to see you back. How come you've chosen America when I'd had thought you might prefer Jerusalem? And while we're at it how do you feel about President

Harrison, or would you have preferred Grover
Cleveland the new tariffs being what they are?"
Apparently, Sitting Bull was getting ready to leave his
camp on Grand River. I asked if we couldn't maybe go
along, though the idea of riding forty miles didn't
appeal. I assumed McLaughlin would refuse but I could
see he thought the whole thing would be carried off
without trouble and to my surprise agreed. I guess, like
many people, he thought a little positive publicity would
be just the thing. Like many people he was wrong. He
told me he would be contacting the military at Fort
Yates, though it would be his police who would make
the arrest. I could see how he didn't want the military to
take the lead whatever Washington might want, and he
was afraid Sitting Bull would escape. We were to take
off right away because otherwise we would miss the
action.

I went back to the cabin. The weather had
improved though it was late in the year with Christmas
almost upon us. I helped her gather her equipment.
Carrying it wasn't going to be easy. Riding forty miles
wouldn't be easy, though thankfully word came that we
would be taken on a wagon. For once I was ahead of the

pack. There were no other reporters and certainly no other photographers so whatever happened we would have a scoop, if arresting an Indian a couple of thousand miles from Manhattan was likely to be of any interest to anyone but the hermit in his apartment.

She was disappointed the interview was off but knew a chance when she saw one. We walked around one another differently than we had, which is to say we were aware that something had happened, but we didn't say anything not to do with where we were going and what we were going to do when we got there. I'd been told the police were leaving from Fort Yates. The idea was that we would set out and meet them, though whether anybody had told them we were coming or not I didn't know. It turned out they didn't. And they didn't like the idea, at all. Later, I saw why.

In case you think a wagon is more comfortable than a horse that's because you have never travelled in one over tracks that disappeared on a regular basis. I remembered as much from that other time and this was certainly no different, though it didn't seem to bother her. She disappeared into herself, doubtless an Indian thing. Where I come from forty miles is a long way.

From one end of Manhattan to the other must be twelve or thirteen miles and I didn't know anyone who had tried it, or wanted to. I once walked the length of Central Park and that was well over two miles. The same from 12th Street to 55th. You can be sure I didn't do that again. Either of them. Out here, forty miles was thought nothing. I was told a horse could manage that easily in a day. Pony Express riders, according to Cody – though I never believed much he told me – could halve that, but they changed horses every ten or fifteen miles. A wagon could only do twenty at best, which is why we needed to leave straight away.

Since nobody wanted us to go no one told us anything. We hired a man who looked as though he could kill us for a dime and set out, not knowing what we would find when we got there, assuming we did since the driver carried a gun at his hip and seemed the kind of man who would use it if you looked at him wrongly, and who knew what that look might be. The idea, though, was that he would only get paid when we came back and since we let him know we didn't carry money with us he had reason to let us live, if reason applied. Of course, we were lying. Where would we have left the money?

As the sun went down, we came to a halt. If I was thinking there would be anything resembling a building, I was wrong. There was nothing resembling anything but land, what people thought they wanted so much they would leave all the marks of civilisation behind. But I suppose most simply moved on figuring that things had to get better somewhere ahead since it was godawful where they were.

At least there were blankets on the wagon, along with some canvas sacks filled with straw. It was bitterly cold, though. He set a fire and cooked something he said were beans, though I couldn't see the similarity. The same went for the coffee which scorched my mouth, though that was probably for the best given its taste. The sensible thing would have been for us to hug each other close – not the driver – but she showed no interest when I suggested it. Which perhaps was as well since she was dressed as a man and who knew what the gunman's views on that score might have been. So, I spent the night shivering and watching the white smear of stars, the moon no more than a sliver, while thinking that

however bad my apartment was it was a damn sight
better than this. Whenever I heard a noise, I figured it
was a snake and, who knows, perhaps it was, even in the
cold. I knew from their snores, though, that the other
two had no such worries, and she did snore which made
me wonder whether I should revise my opinion of her as
a possible bed mate.

Breakfast was beans and coffee, neither of which
had improved overnight. He put the fire out by pouring
the coffee over it. It smelled better that way than in the
pot. We were to set out again before dawn. There was
no one else in sight, as I suppose there wouldn't be.
People talked of wide-open spaces as if they meant
freedom. From what? Decent breakfasts, a daily paper,
streetcars, dentists? I heard how Daniel Boone had
moved on if anyone settled within a hundred miles of
him, which goes to show, though I no more believe a
word they say about him than they do about Custer,
Sitting Bull or Buffalo Bill, most Americans, it seemed
to me, preferring myth over fact, story over history.
Facts don't appeal. They're supposed to in a paper, and
we're taught always to ask someone's age, as if it makes
any difference to know that when the story is about how

302

they fell under a horse or got thrown out of a club. Pinning things down was supposed to matter but just writing what happened can seem very flat. It needs a little colour. While he gathered things together so we could continue, I took her on one side.

'Don't you think it's time you stopped your performance. You make an exceptional woman but a poor man. You are likely to invite more problems as the one than the other.'

'Perhaps I like it.'

'Like it?'

'You think you know me because...'

She stopped, unwilling, perhaps, to name what we had done, what we had become.

'Look, where we are going nobody has seen you. Why not be yourself for once?'

'And you know who you are simply because you wear the same clothes day on day. Incidentally, I have been meaning to mention that before. Where baths are to hand that is one thing. Where they are not, change has its advantages.'

As we climbed into the wagon, I reached out a hand to help her, realising, suddenly, how that might look in a land where men affected a manly distance. She took it nonetheless, though I suspect only to discommode me further.

'We mustn't draw attention to ourselves when we arrive. Photographers need a cloak of invisibility.'

'Really. You think they are so used to someone with a camera that they won't notice you?'

'And if it was a woman with that camera, you think they would see nothing strange? Nonetheless, I will consider it. Men's clothes are abominably uncomfortable, and I have never favoured black.'

With a crack of the whip, we were off. We had barely gone half a dozen miles before the sun rose, pale and watery in a flat December sky which seemed not to have made its mind whether to acknowledge the season. There was no heat in it. High above, a bird circled, though if there was any prey it failed to find it, tilting one wing after hovering for a minute or more, moving off to the west, the faintest of shadows in front.

I was still enough of an easterner to scan the surrounding land half expecting a war party to come riding toward us, but there was nothing there, and plenty of it. The driver spat a black mass of tobacco over the side, except a wind had got up and it hit me in the face. It was no more than I expected, though in truth I have been hit by worse. I still suspected that this was a journey without a point, except maybe it had got one after all, in so far as I had found someone who besides being a pain was also something more, even though she seemed determined not to acknowledge as much.

I asked whether we would arrive before dusk. The answer I got was a cold stare that I found hard to interpret beyond determining not to ask again. In the end, though, the sun had barely disappeared when we came to Sitting Bull's camp. I had expected we might create a stir, but no one seemed to express any interest even when our driver/gunman spat another load of tobacco and this time, it appeared, not altogether randomly it just missing an old woman who stared back at him as if calculating how easily his scalp could be removed.

It seemed word had already arrived that an arrest would be attempted. So much for what passed as security. It turned out a policeman had passed word to a relative telling him to keep out of the way and swearing him to silence, a silence which it appeared had only lasted as long as it took for him to ride into Sitting Bull's camp.

CHAPTER SIXTEEN: THE GHOST DANCER STILLED

Even as we arrived, we could see them dancing. Somehow it seemed pathetic if it meant they had convinced themselves that their time had come again. Their time would never come again. The thing was, though, that whatever energy they had was taken up with dancing around waiting for the Messiah and in truth that didn't seem much of a threat. I couldn't think why McLaughlin was worried, though perhaps it was those back in the east, answerable to those as ignorant as them, who saw this as some last battle. Then there was always Little Big Horn. They had been looking for a chance to wipe that slate clean.

It was bitterly cold when we rode in. The camp itself stretched some four or five miles along the Grand River. To my surprise, Sitting Bull lived in a house, indeed two houses plus a corral, and there was a scatter of log cabins. There were guards around his house. They were carrying rifles.

'Winchesters,' she said, though even I could recognise them. There was a light inside and I could see the shadows of others. If they thought the arrest was going to be straightforward, they were obviously wrong.

'They'll be smoking kinnikinnik,' she said, as we stepped down, and I got ready for another miserable night under the stars. My room back in New York might be stripped of anything that might be considered luxury but freezing to death on the great plains with my only companion someone whose identity seemed to shift with the wind, hardly compared.

'What the hell is kinnikinnik?'

'Something they smoke.'

'I gathered that. Does it have anything to do with tobacco?'

"Maybe, but mostly sumac leaves and the bark of dogwood.'

My tobacco was bad enough, but this sounded terrible. What kind of people were these? I was surprised by the houses, though. I suppose I still thought they lived in wigwams or tepees, never being sure

which, or why anyone would wish to live in either.
Turned out he was better housed than me, but then I
wasn't about to be arrested. This was not a good way to
spend a night less than two weeks before Christmas.

There was no light for photographs, which is
what gives an edge to someone like me, words not
needing overmuch in the way of light. McLaughlin had
told us that whatever happened would be at first light, so
we tried to get a little sleep. There was nowhere to stay
except up against the wagon wondering whether the
beans would mean having to get up in the night.

I couldn't sleep. The guard changed, or a couple
would come out and wander up the trail in the direction
of Fort Yates. So, yes, they knew right enough. And
McLaughlin had counted on surprise. Well, he wouldn't
be the first to make that mistake. Suddenly, someone
was shouting inside the house, but it quickly died down.
Meanwhile, I had lost all feeling in my legs, the cold
creeping up them so that I had to stand and stamp. I
heard the Winchesters being cocked and so sat down as
fast as I had got up. Then the door opened, and they
filed out, joined by the guards. He evidently thought the
danger had passed.

After a moment, Sitting Bull walked across to the corral and got some hay for his horse, the one, I imagined, Cody had given him, the one that could do tricks. The sun chose that moment to rise above a hill down river, shedding a pale light. He walked back to his house, stopped for a moment looking around, and then disappeared inside.

There was little sign of life, except that my companion, who had slipped away, now returned having acquired someone who would explain things to us. He couldn't have been more than sixteen and had ambitions to become a policeman. It was he who identified Bull Head and Shave Head when things got underway.

The young man told us that Sitting Bull had sent his guards away, which we had seen for ourselves. Now it was just a question of waiting and to my surprise nothing happened. After a while people started moving around and, as the day advanced, a few began to dance. This was the chance for photographs. I thought they would object, this being a sacred ceremony, or so I had been told. Maybe she told them she was one of them or spoke to them in their own language. Either way, she spent much of the afternoon taking pictures while I looked around.

I couldn't for the life of me see why this was thought to be the heart of a rebellion. Half the camp was now dancing while the others simply went about their business or sat and smoked what smelt as bad as I assumed it would. McLaughlin was odd. At one moment he treated them as though he were their father or teacher, the next he plotted to stir up trouble where surely there was none. And what would happen to those who were arrested? Were they to be taken to prison or just sent hundreds of miles away?

We spent another night and, as it ended, there were no guards around Sitting Bull's house, and still no police or soldiers, though surely they must already have been on their way. The peace would not last, and just before dawn we heard hoof beats, at first a soft drumming in the ears. Then there was the jingle of harnesses as though a conductor had introduced another instrument to the music of the day.

Even as they rode in my companion who, to my astonishment, had now decided to become a woman again, had set up a tripod and was fixing her camera to it before disappearing under a cloth. The photographs I had seen had all been of people rigidly fixed, as if screwed down to the ground. It didn't seem likely she would be able deal with people fighting one another, if it came to that.

They reined in their horses, and I watched as they entered both houses with no sign of resistance. I waited to see what would happen. In my experience, arrests are usually boring events. Someone is led out. They might shout a little, protest their innocence, even put up a token struggle to show they are serious, but it rarely amounted to anything more than that.

Lights came on inside. If there were no guards outside, it seemed that there were none inside either. By now, people had begun to gather. Obviously, the quicker they finished and were away the better.

A policeman led a horse to the entrance so that I guessed Sitting Bull was to be allowed to ride out. Minutes passed. Perhaps they were having a cup of coffee and a last meal of beans, if my menu was anything to go by. This all looked as though it was going to be a Sunday School picnic with everyone on best behaviour. In the meantime, though, more people had begun to gather and that was something I recognised. Go into a tenement and by the time the cops emerged there would be those ready to hurl whatever came to hand at them as a sign they had no business being there. For the moment, though, they were quiet, ready to take their cue, no doubt, from the man who claimed he was a chief, even as McLaughlin insisted he was not.

The door was wide open, and I could see how Sitting Bull was part naked, trying to struggle into his clothes. Soldiers moved in and out, even as the crowd grew in numbers. After a moment they closed around him and lifted him up, though I couldn't see why since he wasn't resisting. Maybe they had become aware that the thing had to be finished. Now he did begin to fight back. He tried to stop them dragging him through the doorway, planting a leg on each side, this man who had once been a leader of his men, who had ridden around an arena before crowds who whistled and spat before lining up for his signature. They kicked his legs away. Then he emerged between the men who our young

guide identified as Bull Head and Shave Head. Just
behind them was Red Tomahawk which, as names go,
sounded pretty menacing to me.

If they weren't aware of their situation, I was.
There were armed men, growing in numbers with every
minute, and here they were maltreating a man they
revered. One of the policemen punched him repeatedly
in the back with his gun to hurry him on, even as the
crowd closed in. They held onto him as if at any
moment he would break into a run. Women began to
wail and children to cry. The soldiers formed a circle
around him, but were themselves surrounded. There
were enough guns to start a war and perhaps that was
what was about to happen.

I wondered whether they would allow Sitting
Bull to climb on his horse and I could hear a click from
the camera. "Man climbs on horse." That would make a
great headline I thought. Two horsemen appeared, a
blue coated Indian on each.

A man came round the corner of the house.
'Catch the Bear' whispered the young would-be
policeman beside me. Whoever it was carried a

Winchester, but that hardly made him different from anyone else. There was a small army. He took off a blanket and threw it aside, striding forward until he reached the police, bringing his face closer to theirs and prodding them with his rifle like some schoolboy taunting someone he wants to fight. He called something out and one of the policemen got hold of him. There was a sharp click as a cartridge was rammed into the chamber and he pulled away. I couldn't understand what he was saying but he was plainly taunting them, especially the leader.

Suddenly, though, a younger man burst forth, Sitting Bull's son, it turned out, though what he shouted was hardly what a father would look for from a son. What did he say, I asked? From under the black cloth she had draped over herself, she replied, 'If you're so brave how come you, who claimed you would never surrender to blue coats, are now doing so and to Indians in their blue uniforms.' Later, there were those who denied this but that was what she heard, and she spoke the language. Whatever it was, though, it turned out it was all it took to turn things around. It plainly stung Sitting Bull and I watched as he swung around and, after what seemed an age, called something out. He had surrendered before, been arrested before, but clearly had decided to make a last stand, taunted by his own kin it seemed, though heaven knows what he had in mind beyond refusing to go. 'Oh God,' she said, 'he's ordering them to attack.' Even then, there was a click from her camera. She had the instincts of a newspaperman after all.

He was surrounded by those who had been ghost dancing, and I could see how he had made up his mind. He had numbers on his side right enough, but would they step forward? After all, they were immune to bullets. The police pushed him forward in an effort to reach his horse, now saddled and ready. Then he let out a cry. For a second nothing happened. Everyone was frozen in position. What came next was so fast I couldn't follow it at first. Two shots rang out. One at least came from Catch the Bear. The leader of the police, Bull Head as I was later told, and Shave Head, fell. Bull Head was ahead of sitting Bull but the force of the bullet spun him around and, as it did so he fired directly at Sitting Bull. Another shot rang out and Sitting Bull was hit again, this time in the face. All three men fell together as though in a kind of ballet. The shooting was fast, the falling slow. What followed was a confusion of shots, men fighting close up with anything they had to hand. A few ran for the house, and I thought they must be trying to get away, but it turned out they were looking for cover and, once there, started shooting. And all the while the circus horse began to perform its tricks, the noise plainly recalling that of the arena. Though all around men were wrestling and falling, and the air was full of the sound of bullets flying, it went through its routine.

As for myself, I confess my only thought was to find some place I could hide from the general chaos, not having signed on to be shot by one side or the other. I considered running toward the house but since others had already done so, and were firing randomly, I settled for scrambling under the wagon. I hadn't seen our driver since the general warfare started. It was only then, I confess, that I thought of my companion. It turned out that the affection, or whatever it was I felt for her, took second place to my own survival. I looked around and saw she was down. Was she taking cover, or had she been hit.? I hesitated, but could hardly leave her, hoping only that Indians and police were so intent on one another that we would be invisible.

Bullets, though, have no mind of their own and as I crossed toward her, still trying to gauge whether she was alive or not, I felt a tug at my shoulder, no more than that, though I realised I had been hit. An Indian ran across in front of me but paid no notice. He was pursuing a policeman and shot him dead before himself being hit so that he fell, an arm reaching out, though in search of what it was impossible to see.

She still lay as she had when I reached her. I lay down beside her. 'Are you hit?' I asked, hardly expecting a reply, but she turned her head toward me.

'No. I'm fucking dead. Of course I'm not hit. You've heard of lying low. This is what it looks like, as low as I could get. I recommend you do the same.'

'You saw what happened?'

'Of course I saw what happened. My camera. They smashed it.'

'You think that matters? It's a camera.'

She looked at me as though I were saying I didn't care if they killed babies.

'Did you know you're bleeding.'

No, I didn't, but that hardly registered because the battle was all around us. The odds were against the police, outnumbered by almost ten to one. I had seen several crumple and fall but the Indians, those not in blue uniforms, seemed to have discovered that they weren't bulletproof the moment Sitting Bull fell and at last were retreating to the nearby tree line. Then it was over, except for the occasional distant shot. That was when the pain struck home. I let out a cry. She pulled my shirt back.

'It's nothing.'

'Nothing? I've been shot.'

'Mostly you've been missed. A nick.'

'A nick to you, a bullet wound to me.'

'Just needs cleaning up. And my camera's broken. I've got no pictures.'

'Right. Just as well I can still write.'

She tried to spit to clear the dust out of her mouth, but nothing came. Her mouth must have been as dry as mine.

'I need a drink.'

'So do I.'

'Water.'

'Maybe that too.'

I suppose it was the shock because there we were having a fancy conversation while round us people were dead or dying. Bull Head, who was in charge of the soldiers, had been shot, and more than once. They carried him off, heading for the house, while a man tried to hold his innards in, they having turned into outers. Then an Indian was thrown out. It turned out to be Sitting Bull's son. Not that it made any difference, or maybe it did, because they shot him dead straight away. I had seen violence enough back home but nothing like this. It was crude and unforgiving. In the end there was no point to it. The death of Sitting Bull should have marked the end, but instead seemed to have marked the beginning.

The bulletproof shirts had proved useless and by
rights they should have given up right away but there
was a pile of history came before and neither side, it
seemed, could escape its past. The thing was that this
was Indian against Indian, but it was also about what
had happened and what was going to happen. Some had
been tamed, turned around, joining those who had tried
to wipe them out. Others believed there was a game still
to be played when in fact anyone could see it was finally
over. The white men no longer needed to turn up on the
battlefield. All they had to do was dress some other
Indians up in a fancy uniform and issue an order.

It ended as quickly as it started. I counted twelve
dead and half a dozen more on their way to being so. It
turned out that a police uniform was no more able to
protect against bullets than a ghost shirt. McLaughlin
had sent in his own men rather than the military because
he thought they could carry it off without violence.
Well, he got that wrong. As I got to my feet riders were
sent, presumably to fetch the soldiers, but there was no
more fighting. The air had gone out of everyone and
those on both sides stood looking at what they had done
just because someone in Washington decided they

would like things cleaned up when all they had to do was leave things alone. So, they liked dancing and convinced themselves that the good old times were returning. They weren't alone in that. It seemed to me that the older people got the more they longed to turn the clock back thinking people had taken a wrong turn. The nation might be heading west, believing that was the future, but there were those who thought things would never be as good as they were when they were young even if there hadn't been anything they would have been inclined to boast about at the time.

It wasn't long before the soldiers arrived, summoned by someone called Hawk Man No.1. I presume there were numbers 2, 3 and 4 somewhere. For some reason they announced their arrival by sending shells ahead of them so that everyone, including the two of us, ran for cover again. After a while the police raised white flags and the brave soldiers arrived, looking down from their horses at the battle they had missed. What they thought of a scene in which all the dead and injured were Indians I couldn't tell. After all, they had been raised to think that it was whites who were in danger, or why would they have been sent to a place where few if any of them would have chosen to go if offered a choice, the fate of soldiers being that they never are. There was to be no more fighting, the Indians submitting, those closest to Sitting Bull having already ridden out. A lone Indian in the distance rode back and forth daring the soldiers to challenge him no doubt. A few bullets went in his general direction, but he was too far off to be hit. It was as though it were some final ritual designed to mark that it was all over, like the last act of a tragedy.

The scene was a terrible one. I had seen enough dead bodies but never so many gathered in one place. To be truthful, though, my only concern was how to get word back to New York while Jane tried to piece together the camera that would have given her a scoop.

'I can mend it,' she said, as if that made any difference. You have a moment and if you miss it no one is interested.

There was worse ahead, far worse, but for the moment it was a shock. During the battle it had been hard to see what was happening. There was such a melee. The Indian women had picked up whatever they had to hand, knives, clubs, and began beating on the police even as there was a scatter of fire. With my face in the dirt, it was difficult to see anything clearly, but a reporter is supposed to be someone who never looks away, or was that something she had said. Easy to say. Then there was Jane, who I'd thought was hit. This was just a skirmish. For the first time I realised what war must be like with thousands trying to kill one another. I suppose it can't have lasted more than five or ten minutes, enough, though, to leave the dead and dying. Eventually, it had just stopped as if they all suddenly had a sense that there was nothing to do but stop. I found myself shivering. It was cold, but the shivering was from something else. I would have made a bad soldier. I hadn't made too good a reporter.

After a while I saw that Jane was speaking to one of the women. It was not a good moment to be white. The police were Indian, and we had played no role, but it seemed logical they would take against us. After all, who had issued the orders but someone like us. Maybe they recognised something in her. She beckoned me over.

'There's an empty cabin. We can use it.'

'Wouldn't it be better to leave.'

She looked at me oddly.

'Leave? Whatever for? You don't think this is over, do you?'

I rather thought it was, but I was wrong about that, wrong about a lot of things it was turning out. Beyond that, I had stumbled on the biggest story I'd had in a long while.

'I need the telegraph.'

'You go, then. I'm staying.'

She was right. There was more to this story than we had just witnessed, though I couldn't have known what lay ahead.

When I got back, I heard her crying. It was the shock I suppose, or maybe the whole thing brought back memories. I didn't know what to do. Should I reach out to her? Eventually, though, she stopped, and I just lay there in the dark and listened to the sound of women keening somewhere. There was the smell of woodsmoke. Someone rode past, harness jingling. Then there was silence, deep, impenetrable.

We hung on until the funerals, two days later, travelling back, there being no point in staying where we were. The policemen were buried with full military honours at the Standing Rock cemetery, with volleys fired by Captain Milner's entire company of the Twenty-Second Infantry, while the Indians gathered to mourn their own. It was hard to know how to feel. The only people dead were Indians, and we didn't know any of them. It was a bit like the Civil War where everyone was an American and they killed each other, both sides sure they were right. Here, who was in the right? Why didn't they leave Sitting Bull alone? And where was the Messiah? If he'd already come down, he had taken off again, and if they expected him to arrive sometime soon then when he didn't the whole thing would have collapsed. And was Sitting Bull what McLaughlin said he was, this old man who had once charged for pictures of himself? I had read those papers back in Washington and it seemed to me that if I were an Indian I would be angry, but as far as I could see he wasn't about to lead his men into war.

I have a hard time with funerals, but always feel a certain relief that it isn't me about to be buried. I want to cry whether I know the dead person or not, triggered by others. This time I felt nothing. The only thing that stirred with the ripple of gunfire was a flock of birds that lifted into a yellowing sky. Afterwards, people stood around, not knowing quite what to do. This was a military funeral because these men had worn uniforms, but they had not been soldiers and I suspected that those who were, were in two minds about Indians who hadn't stopped being Indians just because they wore uniforms. The whole thing had been a mistake. What was supposed to be straightforward and legal had turned into a bar fight. They would probably hand out medals. It was what happened when mistakes were made. It wasn't only men who had been buried. The whole debacle was to be buried alongside them. Official reports don't favour confessions or ambiguities. They are statements of what was supposed to happen, rather than what did.

There's no logic to history. Someone turns left instead of right; a President goes to the theatre when he could have stayed home. We like to think there is a story to it all when it is one thing and then another with no connection until we choose to say there is. Here, a son taunts his father and, instead of waving him away, the older man shouts out. A man is shot and spins around so that he shoots someone else. What to make of it all? Well, I guess that was down to me. I could say what happened, or what I think I saw happen, and that might make people think it all made sense, when in truth it didn't. That's what stories are. And not just in the papers. Why else do we read books to our children and then again ourselves. We want it all to make sense and if it doesn't then we have ways of shaping it.

I woke up one morning to find her offering me something. I didn't know what it was. Even when I saw it.

'It's a dream catcher,' she said.

'Really. A dream catcher.'

'Yes.'

'That would be what?' I asked, which was not an unreasonable question since it was just a circle of some thin wood, a couple of feathers and a few whisps of something.

'It's Indian.'

'Right. So, it catches dreams?'

'No.'

'Hence the name.'

'You don't want it. Fine.'

'No, it's ... well what does it do then?'

'Keeps you from harm.'

'Not as good as a derringer.'

'All right. Give it back.'

'No. It's, well it's. I like it. But why are you giving it to me?'

'Because it's Christmas day, you ingrate.'

At that I stopped. For the first time in my life, I'd forgotten Christmas. 'Christ,' I said.

'Exactly. Are you Jewish, then?'

'No. I'm not Jewish, I just forgot. What with everything.'

'Yes, well it is. Christmas. So happy Christmas you bastard.'

'I've got nothing for you, except whisky. Would you like some.?'

'It's eight in the morning so, no, I wouldn't.'

'So, happy Christmas. We must do something.'

'Right. What do you have in mind?'

That was a tough question because what could we do in the middle of nowhere, having just watched people killed and buried?

'I don't know, but something. Maybe find something to eat other than beans.'

In the end I found something to give her. I gave her a Waterman pen, though I grant it could leak a little into the cap. I had three with me, though I preferred pencils having had problems filling the pen. It looked fine, though, and seemed to me to beat a dream catcher, but then a dead bat could beat that. She was OK about it. After all, it was Christmas.

By mid-day there were drunk soldiers wandering around, unlike her not running a clock on when to drink. So, we got a bottle out and, after a while, with flakes of snow swirling around, it seemed festive enough. A few drinks in and all was well between us, very well I would say. Somewhere on this great continent, Quakers, Jews, Seventh- day Adventists, Jehovah's Witnesses, atheists, were making a point of not celebrating while back in New York people were buying Christmas trees and baubles on street corners. Some turned to mail order, Tiffany's for the rich, Montgomery Ward for those that weren't. Children were lied to, and this was taken to be a gift, though there would be those who adopted it as a way of life. Well, none of that where we were, and I wished we were back in the snow and slush of Fifth Avenue.

CHAPTER SEVENTEEN: SLAUGHTER

I filed my story, and we could have gone back east but were told the Indians were on the move and it made sense we should consider following them, while having no sense of what lay ahead, because nobody did. Having said that, I don't really know why we thought this a good idea. We had come to talk to Sitting Bull, had failed, but had a bigger story than that would have been. That justified the money. Maybe it was because she never got her pictures that she was the one who argued we should keep going, though what she hoped we would find was a mystery. I was for heading back but if she was staying there was no way I could go.

The military were told to catch those who had left after the shooting, as though they were rounding up strays. Then she was approached to serve as an interpreter. Someone had told someone she spoke Sioux, and it turned out they had no one to hand who could. How crazy could that be? How did they expect anyone to persuade them to come back to the reservation when they'd have to settle for sign language? Apparently some Indian they relied on had chosen to take himself off, and I can't say I blamed him. In the end they never used her, but it was how we got to ride along with those charged to follow those who had left the murder scene – for how else could it be described – and secure their surrender before returning them to the reservation.

So, we followed, riding horses supplied by McLaughlin who, for all he had said there would be no violence if his police were in charge of the arrests, nonetheless seemed pleased with the way things had worked out and was happy for us to file some more stories about how he had brought an end to what he insisted was the risk of insurrection.

And that brings me to what we witnessed there, in the cold of winter, in the last decade of the 19th century, when everyone was talking about the future and here, on the high plains, something happened that drew a final line, civilisation triumphing, it was supposed, but in such a way that made victory feel like defeat, and civilisation a suspect word.

The century was picking up speed. Cities were growing, the country along with them, and there were surely few who cared about the fate of a man who was more myth than reality, but it seemed to me that the man upstairs had maybe been onto something after all. The story of America was the story of the Indian, even if it was also that of men and women of a different colour. Barely a quarter of a century on there were those who still bore the wounds of the Civil War, a war that lacked civility, and what was true of them was true of the country, divided, never quite united. There are cemeteries, north and south, and many who visit them keeping memory alive. But another war had been waged and there were few markers to indicate that a price was paid by those who were required to submit, displaced so others could claim their land, starved, infected, killed, quite as if history required their sacrifice. Had I thought any of this before? Of course not. Would any of this make its way into the *Telegraph*? It would not. Though what happened in this place beside a creek, as one year edged toward another, would change me, and the photographs she took here would, for the moment, and who knows perhaps forever, fix this place in the minds of those who saw them. But then again, time moves on and yesterday's news is no longer news

We rode with the Seventh cavalry. The aim, we were told, was to intercept Big Foot and his followers as they moved from the Cheyenne river in the direction of the Bad Lands. It seemed he was heading toward Pine Ridge Agency. Eventually we came upon them some twenty miles from there. I expected a fight, but nothing of the kind occurred. Indeed he, or one of those who followed him, raised a white flag. I presumed that meant there would be talks and Jane would come into her own, but Major Whitside showed no interest, and they were required to surrender. I thought they might resist but, instead, they capitulated and were moved on northeast of Pine Ridge.

By this stage I was thoroughly saddle sore so that when I dismounted it was painful to walk. It was also getting colder by the moment. New York is cold enough but at least you can step into a steam-heated building. Here there was no protection.

Suddenly, there were soldiers everywhere. Big Foot and his followers didn't seem to number much more than a couple of hundred. Along with the men were women and children. They appeared peaceable enough to me, but obviously the military were taking no chances. They even had artillery which arrived bouncing up and down behind horses flecked with saliva. Artillery?

'Hotchkiss,' she said.

'Hotchkiss?'

'A one pounder.'

What did I know. She was the expert when it came to guns.

'Five barrels.'

'Five?'

'Sixty-eight rounds a minute.'

'And why would they need those?'

'Because they're going to kill them all.'

At the time that sounded like nonsense, but it seemed she knew about military tactics as well as guns. I lost count of the numbers of soldiers, but it was many times those they surrounded.

The night was as cold as any I have experienced, and I was glad to be up and about convinced that

movement would unfreeze my fingers and toes. I can
tell you; it takes more than movement. Looking down
on the camp at first light I could see there was still a
white flag. The tepees were in the open. On the other
side was a ravine that ended up in a creek The soldiers
were on all sides and the Hotchkiss guns lined up. I
counted four of them. Just before eight a group of
soldiers, along with Indian scouts, rode in and
dismounted.

   She had set up her camera further forward than I
would have been inclined to go but having failed to
capture any pictures of Sitting Bull was determined to
record something this time, even if it was only a bunch
of Indians laying down their rifles, which is what they
were ordered to do, though as far as I could see they
only produced a couple of them. There was no sign of
Big Foot but apparently he was ill. I could see how the
soldiers were going through the tepees and eventually
they piled some two dozen rifles on the ground. I guess
rifles were about the only things they owned, apart from
their horses. I saw how one of them started dancing, but
he was on his own. There was a pathos to it. They must
have seen that the promises had turned to nothing. Then

some sort of argument broke out, except I couldn't tell
over what, being too far off. One of them seemed to be
struggling with two soldiers, holding onto his rifle.
Suddenly there was a shot. I guess it was from that same
rifle. A second later there was a volley, it seemed from a
group of Indians though I couldn't be sure. Maybe the
first shot was a sign. It made no sense. What were a
handful of them going to do in the face of hundreds of
soldiers, though maybe they still thought their shirts
would protect them despite what had happened to
Sitting Bull? That was all it took. A moment later and
the soldiers started firing.

I could see where the Indians tried to grab their
rifles from where they were piled and a few of them
managed it, shooting back, but the Hotchkiss opened up
and people started falling, some of them soldiers. I saw
Jane crouching down, afraid she was in the line of fire
even as women ran in and out of the tepees with a
straggle of children, heading toward the ravine. Half a
dozen soldiers on horseback cut across in front of me,
stones spitting out. They were firing as they rode. I saw
where a woman ran forward towing a child except that
she dropped suddenly, shot through as I guessed. The

child clung to her but it, too, became still even as the rest of the scene was a swirl of movement. There was a haze of blue smoke from the guns.

I looked behind me and saw where an officer sat still in his saddle, looking down and making no move to stop it. Aside from the few who had rushed to get to their guns, all the Indians were unarmed as far as I could see. I guess they must have had their knives and tomahawks but what could they do against the regular thump of the Hotchkiss, the rattle of rifle fire, bullets like rain.

Men on horses chased down those trying to escape. How long did it last? Time seemed to stand still. Maybe it was half an hour, maybe more. To tell the truth, I have no idea. When most of the shooting had stopped there were still soldiers wandering around shooting the wounded, while in the distance there was sporadic firing as those that had run were caught and dispatched. Then it was finally over. I was numb, and not just from the cold, though a few flakes of snow drifted down.

I ran down to Jane. Her camera was on the ground beside her. She was shaking.

'Are you OK?' I asked.

'OK?' she said looking at me as though I were a fool.

In some ways the silence was worse than the clatter, rattle, thunder of the guns, the smoke from which had now cleared on the wind. Every now and then there was the distant noise of guns, but after a while even that stopped. We didn't go down into the camp, an officer wheeling his horse and blocking our way. He had a blank face as if even he couldn't make sense of things. I certainly couldn't. You see things with your own eyes and still don't register it.

Down below, the ground was littered with bodies. I thought of a line from Dante. 'I had not thought that death had undone so many, 'and that after he and Vergil had passed through the gate of hell with its inscription 'Abandon hope, ye who enter here.' Something had died here beyond those who lay on what was not a battlefield but a sudden mortuary. It seemed even the dogs had been shot. Why they had done this was beyond me. Perhaps when the blood cooled it would be beyond those who had killed with such wildness. Or maybe this was no more than revenge, though it was fifteen years since Little Big Horn, which is a long while to wait.

I was used to death, but this was something else. I had never been close to a battle but even I knew this was not a battle. One group of people simply set out to destroy another group of people, evidently not counting them as such. I had seen how men and women had run around looking for safety they would never find. When I was young, I had a cat for a while. The idea was that it would catch mice in the barn. Instead, it caught birds, not killing them at first, letting them go for a second or so, making them think they might get away. Then it pounced. When they were dead, it came indoors and laid them in front of me before walking away. They had no interest except in the killing. Perhaps there had been a time when they and their kind had done this for food, but that time had long gone. Now they killed because that was what they did. I had just watched soldiers kill and then ride on, maybe because that was what they did.

341

That was all it took. And there were the bodies, laid out like so many broken and destroyed birds.

There are some things that get lost in the telling, some things that can't be captured in words, though that's supposed to be my job. Worse things happened at Antietam and Shiloh, many thousand dead, but I wasn't there and there were soldiers on both sides. One or other claimed victory, and I could be sure the army would here, except it didn't look any more like victory than it did back in Chicago where I'd learned it took thirty-five minutes to turn a living cow into dead meat.

Jane pressed up against me for the cold that night. I was told the Lakota called it The Moon of the Popping Trees since you could hear the twigs snapping in the freezing wind, not that there were any trees here. I woke more than once hearing her crying. I couldn't be sure whether she was awake or dreaming, one nightmare blending into another. In the morning I helped her with her camera. It turned out she wasn't the only photographer. There was someone, I was told, called George Trager. She went ahead, nonetheless. I could see how upset she was, but she went about her business with a kind of cold determination. She was no longer just a photographer. She was collecting evidence, like a detective, like a pathologist, like a reporter.

We stayed on a couple of days. This was news and I was a newsman. There were other reporters, but they weren't from anywhere that bothered me. There was someone from the Omaha Daily Bee, and a William Kelley of the Lincoln State Journal, along with a man called Charlie from the Chadron Democrat, which I gathered was somewhere in Nebraska. This was news to them because they came from here or hereabouts. Later, we shared a bottle or two since I didn't see them as rivals. Nonetheless, I rushed off to telegraph a piece, leaving Jane behind. Later, when I got back east, though, I found that the *Herald* had had a piece in their European edition on New Year's Eve, but it was no more than a hundred words or so, and who cares about Europe.

It would be just after New Year that we left. But we had seen enough that first day and the ones that followed. We walked around the camp, and out along the ravine which was no more than a dark slash in the earth. It was where those who ran were shot down, mothers, children, babies included. The thin branches of

the tepees were still standing, stark skeletons. A few
horses were scattered around, those who once rode them
no more than smudges against the white of a thin snow.
It struck me that this was where it all ended, the battle
for land, for the future, a history that wasn't history
because it wasn't written down by those who were
broken as you would a horse. There were some
survivors who were gathered together, but every now
and then that first day there had been a pistol shot, sharp
and clear as, I suspected, some of the wounded were
dispatched or, I can only hope, some injured horse.

One young soldier came up to us. He was pale
and shaking. Jane looked up at him and it seemed to be
the trigger for him to start crying. It turned out he had
seen where a woman had been shot dead, but her baby
had continued to suckle. Not for long, though, it having
a wound of its own. I took a note but doubted this was a
story anyone would want to read.

By New Year they had started collecting the
bodies loading them onto carts, some frozen as they had
fallen, one man reaching out his hand, pointing at the
sky, though what he was looking for who can know.
Maybe he was calling on God as a witness, though God

had obviously turned his face away. The men carrying the dead were not soldiers, more like cowboys if I really knew what such looked like beyond the pictures in dime novels. Someone pointed out Big Foot. He was lying on his back, a thick coat on and a shawl over his head. His hands were out to the side. He could have been sleeping if anyone would choose to sleep on the frozen ground. I couldn't see where he had been hit. He was like a fallen statue, a smother of snow on his lower half, his top almost clear.

There was another who for some reason has stayed with me. He was dead alright, a crust of blood catching the low sun so that for a second it was like a small cluster of rubies in the middle of his forehead. His eyes were open, filmed over with ice. But what struck me especially was that his hand was missing a finger. Why, when there was nothing but a general carnage, did that seem important? I have no idea. Even so, there have been nights when I have woken from a dream in which he looked at me with his frosted eyes as though he would understand something, that I had the answer to a question he could never ask and that I could never answer.

Along with the bodies they seemed to be collecting souvenirs, a ghost dance shirt, a war club. I saw a man take a necklace, or some such, from the neck of woman whose child lay beside her, a dusting of snow oddly softening the horror. Other soldiers strolled among the dead with a curiously disinterested air as if they had come across some phenomenon in nature. High in the sky a bird flew in wide circles. It seemed there were a lot of birds looking for food. I guess it didn't matter over much to them whether it was alive or dead.

Soldiers had started digging a trench up where the Hotchkiss guns had been. Others, all holding rifles, stood around and watched as the bodies were thrown in on top of one another. Others were piled up waiting their turn. There were two men down below, both wearing hats, one with a waistcoat. It wasn't a ceremony. They were disposing of people as my father once buried meat that had gone off.

There were solders who had died, though it was hard to believe that most of them had been shot by the Indians, the firing being so haphazard with the camp surrounded so that bullets fired from one side must have hit those on the other. I never heard an order to shoot but this hadn't been a disciplined army, not for the time it took to wipe out everyone they could.

We left. It had just been a bit of land in the middle of other land that would have meant nothing to anybody but for the thing that had happened. What people would make of it depended on who told the story. You could be sure the army would have its version, and nobody would ask the Indians, most of whom were beyond being asked anything. A while after I got back someone sent me a letter with a clip from a paper in Aberdeen, South Dakota. It declared that 'our only safety depends upon the total extermination of the Indians. Having wronged them for centuries, we had better, in order to protect our civilizations, follow it up by one more wrong and wipe these untamed and untameable creatures from the face of the earth." There was another piece, written after Sitting Bull died. It said, "Sitting Bull, most renowned Sioux of modern history, is dead. He was an Indian with a white man's spirit of hatred and revenge for those who had wronged him and his. With his fall the nobility of the Redskin is extinguished and what few are left are a pack of whining curs who lick the hand that smites them. The

Whites, by law of conquest, by justice of civilization, are masters of the American continent, and the best safety of the frontier settlements will be secured by the total annihilation of the few remaining Indians." So, there it was. We had won and they had lost. We had won because we stood for civilization. That made me think of Twain's Huck Finn who complained that he had been civilized before and didn't think much of it. Right then, I didn't either.

CHAPTER EIGHTEEN: THE END OF SOMETHING

Those newspaper cuttings didn't mean anything to me at the time beyond how wrong someone who wrote for the papers could be. Ten years later I read about a book for children called *The Wizard of Oz* by the same man who had written for the papers out in South Dakota, calling for the extermination of the Indians, L. Frank Baum. I got hold of a copy and read where he had said, 'No matter how dreary and grey our homes are, we people of flesh and blood would rather live there than in any other country, be it ever so beautiful. There is no place like home.' Well, those who survived the fight in a place that was as dreary and grey as you could hope to find, certainly never had a home again and even ten years on I could see how what had happened meant that in some way we didn't either because something got lost. It turned out that the man who sat above the store and told me that the story of America was the story of America was not wrong. It was just that the story was one that could stain the soul.

Anyway, I travelled back with Jane. She had been shaken up by it all. So had I, but I wasn't part Indian. At first, she hardly spoke, but the further we went the more she began to relax. She had changed back into a woman which made life easier, for me at least. Did I say easier? What I mean is that my feelings became clearer. Back there she had clung to me not because of the cold but out of fear or shock. Now when she leant against me, as the train swayed and jolted, it was something else, though there was something between us. That something was what we had seen.

We stopped off in Chicago long enough for me to telegraph a follow up story, though it was hard to know if there was likely to be any interest. And sure enough, when I got back, I found they had published my first story but thereafter there was more interest in a cow born with two heads in Pennsylvania, a fire in the Bronx, a man who murdered his whole family and then mailed them in parts to his relatives, along with the usual pieces about aldermen caught with the wrong woman on the eve of elections.

It turned out the *Times* had published the army's version, though it mentioned dead women and children.

In February, they let Indians tell their version but the
next day their headline was 'Colonel Forsyth
Exonerated: His Action at Wounded Knee Justified,"
saying he had been restored to command of what it
called his 'Gallant Regiment,' And that was it. Medals
were awarded, The Medal of Honor going to twenty of
those who lacked a particle of honor between them.

It was then I received a call and climbed the
stairs to where I knew a man would still be sitting in
front of a fire, this time with good reason since it was
freezing out on the streets, snow piled high along the
sidewalks. Outside our building a horse had slipped and
couldn't get up. The ice was dyed lime green where it
had pissed in fear, scarlet from a wound in its side.

I knocked as loud as I dared. There was no
response. I knocked again. It occurred to me that he was
pretty old so maybe could be dead. At last, there was a
sound, a kind of high-pitched, wavering cry, and I went
in. Time seemed to have stood still. He was where I had
seen him last. Well, that's to say I couldn't see him,
hidden by the high wings of his leather chair. A white
hand appeared and waved me forward. Though there
was a fire, a window was open, and a flurry of snow

blew in over the top of a huge iron radiator as though a battle were being waged between heat and cold.

'Sit,' he said.

He was paler than I remembered, though a flare of flame lit his face. He was wearing eyeglasses and they shone orange for a moment. I sat. And waited. And waited. I thought perhaps the effort of saying a single word had worn him out.

At last, he spoke. 'The Indians.'

What else. 'The Indians,' I replied, recalling my former strategy.

'So.'

'So' I ventured.

'You were there.'

Since he had sent me, and I had filed a story, that seemed an odd remark. 'I was,' I confirmed, adding 'there' just to be clear.

'I read about it in the *Times*.'

The *Times*? Did he not read his own paper?'

'I wrote a piece.'

'In the *Times*?' he queried.

So, he had finally lost it if he hadn't long since. 'No. For us.'

'Oh, I read that, of course. So, what did you really think?'

'Like I said in the piece.'

'I told you.'

'You told me,' I said, trying not to let it sound like a question, not being sure what he was talking about.

'The Indian,' he replied.

'Ah, yes. The Indian.'

'That's the real history of this country.'

'This country,' I echoed.

'Ended, then.'

History? The Country? The Indians?

'Did they fight back?'

'Some.'

'Washington,' he said, 'the military.'

I couldn't think of what to say. He was silent again and then said, 'I read them.'

'Read them,' I tried.

'Your other pieces.'

So, the pieces they didn't run.

'Slaughtered,' you said.

'Well …'

'Wiped out. Women and children.'

'Pretty much.'

'Pretty much?'

'Well, yes, wiped out.'

'Why was that?'

Why? 'A mistake, maybe. Panic?

'A mistake, you think.'

354

'Maybe.'

'You going to say it was a misunderstanding? That was no misunderstanding. That was planned. In the stars.'

In the stars? Then, nerving myself, I asked, 'Why didn't you run them? The other pieces?'

He sat still for a moment and then leaned forward, even as there was another spurt of flames as a log shifted in the grate. His glasses made it look as though his eyes were red and he some tormented figure from hell.

'No need,' he said, raising his paper-white hand, 'It was over. It had worked itself out. The final battle. Now we know.'

I wanted to ask what it was that we knew but I could see he thought I was a poor audience.

'We know what lies ahead. Not enough we have one curse. Now we have another. First the slaves, then the Indians. There'll be a price to pay. They closed it, you know.'

355

Closed what? I was beginning to wonder whether I could edge out before he foamed at the mouth.

'The frontier. They closed it. Nowhere to go now. Too many graves. Can't go west, can't go south.'

Closing the frontier seemed a pretty good idea to me. As to the South, it was a foreign country. and I was happy for it to stay such.

'Well,' I said, meaning to add 'I should be going,' except good sense and the need for a job meant I couldn't say that.

'You think the end times are here?'

'The end of …'

'Everything. That's what they thought. I guess not.'

At least he was answering his own questions.

'You want to know why I didn't run your other pieces? There was no need. You had said it. We must move on. Know where the future lies?'

Ahead? I thought to say, but he no longer needed me.

'In Rochester.'

'Rochester?'

'And West Orange, New Jersey.'

I was unsure where the future would lie, but Rochester and West Orange seemed unlikely places for anything.

'So, Rochester and West Orange.'

'George Eastman and Edison. Film. Moving film.'

So, the future wasn't the Indians anymore. The Indians had gone. What about the curse, then? And what was moving film?

'They've got something called a Kinetograph.'

'Really. And the Indians?'

'The Indians?'

'You said they were the story of America.'

'They were, son, but that story ended. You wrote about it.'

'And the curse?'

'You think we could do what we did and not
pay? We'll pay. We'll go on paying, but there's a new
century coming, and that's the story we've got to start
telling.

'You didn't use her photographs.'

'Her?'

'His. The Photographs.'

'They didn't move, son. Your words were
better.'

'They were massacred.'

He was silent and after a moment or two sank
back in his chair. At last, he spoke, but I could tell he
was tiring.

'You saw history, son. You saw the end of
something. You saw what we would do to own the
future. Somebody always pays for a dream and it's the
dreamer. Well, it's done. The blood has been spilled. It
won't be the last. But I guess you have something to do.
Did I mention I didn't approve of you claiming a gun on
expenses.

EPILOGUE

The year 1901 began with the release from jail
of Alferd Packer, having served eighteen years for
cannibalism. Happy New Year. In April, one of my
favourite authors, O. Henry (real name William Sydney
Porter) was also out of prison, having served three years
for embezzlement. So, good news for them, though not
so good for the President of the United States who, on
visiting the Pan-American Exposition in Buffalo,
offered to shake hands with Leon Czolgosz, an
anarchist, who did what anarchists do. He shot him
dead, with a .32 calibre Iver Johnson revolver, Johnson
being a man who also made bicycles and should perhaps
have restricted himself to those. Czolgosz was executed
by electricity, which was only right since the Exhibition
had been powered by that through cables going to
Niagara Falls, though I doubt he saw the
appropriateness. It was also the year that the five tribes
– the Choctaw, Cherokee, Seminole, Chickasaw, and
Creek – were recognised as US citizens even as they
were forced to leave their land, handing over 14 million
acres to whites. I had long since left Wounded Knee

behind but had never forgotten what had happened there. So, the new century carried forward the work of the previous one. And I had changed. Who would not have done who had been there when the sound of Hotchkiss guns had signalled the end of any idea of our innocence, of the New Eden we had told the world was where we lived?

And what of the woman who tended to dress as a man? Well, she does so no longer, which is just as well since people might look at me strangely if she did, we now being married and with a daughter whose name is Zuya, which in the Sioux language means warrior woman, and you can guess whose idea that was.

Meanwhile, my old boss is long dead, though it had taken a week or more before anyone realised, the building being plagued with rats so that we were all accustomed to the smell from those which had inconveniently expired in the hollow walls. My God if he didn't leave some of his money to an Indian school, the rest going to someone who wanted to re-bury Abraham Lincoln evidently thinking that those who did the job the first time around had fallen short of requirements. And it turned out he wasn't wrong about moving film. There was even one about the Indian school made by something called the American Mutoscope and Biograph Company, though that was being sued by Edison over patents, lawyers being the true inheritors of the earth.

His role was taken over by a man who always dressed in black and who, with eyeglasses perched on the bridge of his nose, looked more like a haberdasher than newspaper owner. He never mentioned Indians, no longer lived above the store, and left us all pretty much alone which was fine with me because I was now the editor, no longer required to visit the morgue, meet lowlifes in back allies, fetch ham on rye, that being a distant memory.

Though, as a nation, we prefer to regard the past as best forgotten, there are some echoes hard to ignore. The city was a mass of people, wandering the streets, drinking in bars, encamped in Central Park, smoke rising from fires. Despite the cold, they still arrived, by train, on carriages, walking or marching. Blue was the predominant colour -- though the clouds hung low, and the buildings were dull, there being no sun to prompt reflections -- because this was what distinguished the uniform of an army that had sought to turn the world around.

The other colour was grey, that of other uniforms taken out of trunks where they had been neatly folded away to be unfolded once a year to recall not so much what happened as what they believed had happened. The strange thing was that they were happy to drink with each other, if occasionally this ended in half-hearted blows.

Every year they parade through the streets, one lot celebrating a victory, the other a defeat they will not accept was a defeat. I watched them pass from my office high above the street, a fire, I admit, flickering in the grate since I had chosen to move my office up the stairs I had once climbed wondering what madness I would encounter there.

Then, for no reason I could understand, there appeared a horse, and on it an Indian in full headdress. It stopped right below my window and the Indian looked up quite as though he could see me, even as heavy flakes of snow drifted down, already settling, the grey city street slowly disappearing as the snow sparkled silver in the light from the city's gas lamps. Then, slowly, the horse rose on its rear legs, stationary, as in the distance I could hear music filtered through the night air. Then it lowered itself and bowed down as though to an invisible audience. A moment more and it had gone, if it was ever there, me having had a glass or two, and maybe more. The new century, we are told, and the *Telegraph* tells its readers, is bright with possibility. Somewhere in the city people were watching moving pictures, wondering about what men could do. The sins of the past, it seems, are to be forgotten. Not by me, though. Not by me.

Printed in Great Britain
by Amazon

86147595R00210